Last Shot

The last shot was so simple—a car driving away from Notre-Dame-de-la-Garde, high above Marseille. The unit had been disbanded and the Director had already flown to Hollywood, leaving the camera-crew and pretty Joanna, Production Coordinator (general dogsbody), to take care of it.

Yet within minutes of getting the scene in the can a Mercedes is forcing Joanna's little Renault off the autoroute, men are trying to grab her in the airport, her hotel room is torn apart.

Why? Joanna knows that multi-millionaire Monsieur Laurent has for months been attempting to stop the film—he claims it libels his family. Yet would he go as far as murder? Somebody does. And the only person Joanna can turn to for help in this alien city is charming Marc, with whom she has already had a brief love-affair.

But is Marc the honest young man he seems to be? And why is the last shot so interesting to the lovely mistress of Leo Nogaro, who runs Marseille, inefficiently, on his father's behalf?

The Nogaros can exact the death-penalty when and as they wish, and they certainly wish to kill Joanna and Marc, but . . . but those two have by now hidden the last shot where no one can find it, for it represents not only their Life Insurance but a potential crock of gold.

by the same author

LOADED QUESTIONS
DEATH WISHES
SEA-CHANGE
ASK THE RATTLESNAKE
VOICES IN AN EMPTY ROOM
PHOTOGRAPHS HAVE BEEN SENT TO YOUR WIFE
W.I.L. ONE TO CURTIS
DAY OF THE ARROW
A MAFIA KISS

PHILIP LORAINE

Last Shot

COLLINS, 8 GRAFTON STREET, LONDON W1

William Collins Sons & Co. Ltd
London · Glasgow · Sydney · Auckland
Toronto · Johannesburg

First published 1986
© Philip Loraine 1986

British Library Cataloguing in Publication Data

Loraine, Philip
  Last shot.—(Crime Club)
  I. Title
  823'.914[F]   PR6062.067

  ISBN 0 00 231431 2

Photoset in Linotron Baskerville by
Rowland Phototypesetting Ltd
Bury St Edmunds, Suffolk
Printed in Great Britain by
William Collins Sons & Co. Ltd, Glasgow

ONE: CLOSE-UP—JOANNA

1

On Wednesday 18 April at two o'clock in the afternoon Joanna Sorensen started running; she was to go on running for three days. And it all began merely because she was doing her job to the best of her ability.

92. EXT. MARSEILLE—NOTRE-DAME-DE-LA-
    GARDE. DAY.   92.

Steven, irritated and disturbed, comes quickly out of the church, looking for Danielle. No sign of her. He goes to the edge of the terrace (sea and city, Old Port and the docks beyond, laid out at his feet).

Movement makes him glance downwards.

93. STEVEN'S P.O.V. to road below Notre Dame.   93.
Danielle's white Alfa-Romeo shoots out of the parking-lot. CAMERA PANS with it as it accelerates down the steep street, Montée de l'Oratoire, and disappears around a corner

94. CLOSE-UP—STEVEN. Irritation is swept away   94.
by surprise and doubt. Why has she abandoned him here alone?

He looks to left and right, suddenly tense, touched by an intimation of danger. Then turns and goes leaping

down the steps away from this place which, he is now
sure, has become some kind of trap.

Location-shooting on *The Sleeping Dog* (working title)
finished two days before, the 16th. The unit which had,
until that moment, seemed immutable, bound together by
steel cables of professionalism and common endeavour,
flew apart and disintegrated. Joanna was now used to the
phenomenon but could never forget how much it had
startled her on first encounter four years ago: even though
it was part of her job to organize the dispersal. People who
had seemed to be firm friends for life suddenly vanished into
thin air amid fading echoes of farewell. In this case some of
them would resume relationships in ten days' time when
studio-shooting began in England; others might never be
seen again. Had there really been comradeship, even friendship, even intimacy? Perhaps not; just the old illusion known
as show-biz.

The Producer was already in New York, raising yet
another million dollars to add to a top-heavy budget. The
Director, final 'Cut' hardly out of his mouth, was flying
directly to Los Angeles in order to ensure that the Studio
heard his version of events before anyone else's. The Stars,
barely on speaking terms anyway, had flown East and West
respectively: she to India where her next picture was being
prepared, he to his much-publicized ranch in Arizona, there
to commune with his much-publicized herd of long-
horns. ('He probably speaks their language, dear,' was his
co-star's alleged exit line, 'he sure as hell can't speak
English!')

These departures, and a hundred more, Joanna had
supervised in person: part of her job as Production Co-
ordinator, smart new title for the old Production Secretary,
still a general dogsbody whatever they called her.

'Hey, Jo?' the Director had said, lounging into her office
prior to take-off. He knew she hated the name, and had

never missed an opportunity of calling her by it since she had given him the sexual brush-off in no uncertain terms, *and* after he'd taken the trouble to dine her at some memorable Michelin three-star. 'Hey, Jo? There's just the one scene up there at the church. After the sonofabitch has run out looking for the girl—his p.o.v. to her car.'

'Yes, Mr Rocca. Scene ninety-three.'

He had been trying to get her to call him Nelson since long before the brush-off, but no sir! Always this 'Mr Rocca' and a cool grey Connecticut/Scandinavian look to go with it, informing him that as far as she was concerned Nelson was a British admiral who had defeated the French at Trafalgar and died of it.

'Guess I can leave that to you and Tom, huh?'

Since Tom, the cameraman, had won five Oscars during his long working life, and could have directed the whole picture standing on his head while playing a game of Scrabble, Joanna didn't need to answer this one; the cool grey look was enough.

'You'd better pan with the car. And maybe try a zoom towards the end of the pan—might make a good cut.'

Joanna, product of UCLA film-school, considered the zoom a pointless cliché which would certainly end up on the cutting-room floor, but did not say so; instead, 'Sure, Mr Rocca. Tom and I can make quite a production out of that.'

The Director discarded several witty replies before shrugging and turning towards Los Angeles.

So the unit went its several ways, leaving Production Co-ordinator, camera crew, and the French Second Assistant to garner this last relatively unimportant shot on the following day. But on the following day the Mistral, that ill wind, burst out of its alpine lair and came knifing down the Rhône Valley, driving squalls of rain in front of it; the people of Marseille turned their customary bile green and were blown hither and thither, giving each other bilious looks;

easy to understand why the Mistral caused murder.

Joanna played poker with the camera crew, and lost, and drank too much Scotch, and went early to bed because the forecast for the next day, that memorable Wednesday the 18th, promised fair weather by mid-morning.

Sure enough, and as unlikely as it seemed, at eleven o'clock the clouds were sundered into vast black chunks and the sun came flashing forth in Mediterranean splendour; the barbarian north wind, face to face with its old enemy, howled in anger, veered, and fled blustering back to the mountain snows. Suddenly it was hot.

Joanna and the camera crew, who had been shuddering in their parkas on the south side of Notre-Dame-de-la-Garde, perched on its rock high above the city, returned to the shrouded and waiting camera. While they uncovered it and made meticulous adjustments Joanna flicked on her walkie-talkie: 'Marc?'

'Jeanne—how are you, is it cold up there?' The voice of the Second Assistant cut through her professional resolve and decapitated her authority. God damn him! So he was attractive, so were a lot of other men, so what! On the other hand it was very nice not to be called Jo. He never had: always Jeanne with a soft J.

'We're going. Are you ready?'

Through the walkie-talkie she heard the car start up a hundred feet below. Marc said, 'Ready.'

'The extras?'

'They will move when I signal.'

'Police?'

'Standing by. Traffic is already stopped.'

Tom, the old cameraman, had checked with his crew. He now looked at the girl politely and with affection: so very feminine in her mannish, modish clothes: black windcheater, tight black jeans tucked into smart black boots; she was twenty-five, the same age as his favourite grand-daughter, but she was nominally in charge of this operation, and he well knew how easy it was to scrape the young on their raw inexperience.

Young or not, she knew the business. 'Okay, let's go.'

'Speed,' from the camera assistant. Johnny, the clapper-boy was there with his board which proclaimed, '*Sleeping Dog*. Scene 93, Take 1.'

Joanna said, 'Action.' Immediately she knew it was no good. The twelve extras toiled up the slope towards the church, as rehearsed, but the white car was almost out of sight before the camera had even reached the parapet edging the terrace. 'Cut.'

Old Tom shook his head. 'What *is* it about cars? They're . . . No. I was going to say they're more trouble than actors, but that's impossible.'

The car drove back into the parking-lot. Other drivers and a few impatient pedestrians who had been held up by the police were allowed to go about their business. The extras returned to their allotted positions. Into her walkie-talkie Joanna said, 'Marc?'

'I know, I know.'

'Hold the car when I say "Action", let it go when I say "Car".'

He replied in French. She couldn't speak the language but understood him perfectly; he had said, 'You are as intelligent as you are beautiful.'

'*Sleeping Dog*. Scene 93, Take 2.' It went perfectly. The camera moved to the edge of the terrace and tilted downwards in perfect synchronization with the action of the leading man, already filmed; the car shot into view; the camera swiftly panned with it past dark pine-trees and picturesque red roof-tops until it disappeared around the corner.

Old Tom said, 'Nice! One more for luck?'

'One more,' said Joanna, 'with the maestro's lovely zoom. Sorry about that.'

The camera crew all laughed. Into the walkie-talkie she said, 'Marc? Again.'

'That was not good?' He too was a professional, he was affronted.

'No, it was perfect. The Director wants one with a zoom.'

'This will be called The Zoom-Zoom Movie.'

'They'll all be cut.'

'I hope. Are you warmer now?'

'Yes, quite a change. We'll be a few minutes while they fit the lens.' She did not intend to chat with him. He, knowing that her unwillingness only indicated the continuing attraction towards him which she disowned, said happily, 'Zoom-zoom!' and switched off. Then, of course, she realized how much she had *wanted* to chat with him; like this, safely, a hundred feet of sheer drop dividing them.

The camera operator, an individual of great charm and wit, gave her a sly glance. Well, she had to expect that; nothing was ever hidden from a film unit; it seemed that everybody had known about her brief affair with the charming young Frenchman almost before she knew about it herself. No criticism and no ill-will, naturally; such things were part of their febrile professional life, as quickly forgotten as all the rest of it. But not by her.

Old Tom, perceiving the hidden and fleeting embarrassment (but then there was nothing about women that his cinematic eye did not perceive), softened the moment by saying, 'You're wasted, you ought to be in front of my camera. What I couldn't do with those cheekbones!' He had said it before, and it was no idle compliment; he had photographed too many famous faces to be bothered with compliments.

She smiled. 'You wouldn't think that when you saw my acting.'

'Oh, acting!' He knew that his beloved camera could, and did, do seventy-five per cent of the acting. He took the perfect young face in one gnarled and gentle hand, turning it so that the ash-blonde hair half hid it, wind-blown; he squinted at her, wrinkled lids almost closed. There was not a trace of sensuality in any of this. 'The eyes change colour too. In this light, facing the sea, they're blue.'

'Okay, Jo,' said the operator, 'ready. Tom, stop handling the goods!'

'Old men,' replied his superior, 'are allowed to handle the goods. Right—as before, but with boring and unnecessary zoom. Start when the car passes the woman in black.'

'Scene 93, Take 3.' Speed. Action. Car. Zoom. Cut. It all went perfectly. Old Tom said, 'Who needs directors?' They shot a fourth take without zoom, just in case; and that was the end of their day's work, end of location filming on *The Sleeping Dog* (working title).

2

It was now that things, which Joanna was to recall later, began to happen. But how little one is ever able to recall later!

As soon as they reached the car park at the foot of the steep bluff on which Notre-Dame-de-la-Garde stands she realized that her eyes were searching for Marc Gérard; absolutely unbidden, they searched, as eyes will when under the influence of love or desire or whatever name their owners can bring themselves to accept, or, in Joanna's case, not accept. She was furious with the eyes but unable to control them. There he was, over on the far side of the parking-lot, talking to a shady-looking character in dark glasses, local mafia by the look of him.

She did not at this point see the silver Mercedes, and yet it must have been there, or near. Certainly she was being watched: by some two dozen of the people who always, in any weather in any place, mysteriously appear to gape at a film unit. She was used to this, however, and paid them scant attention: particularly since the three grey lawyers who had been dogging their footsteps for the past six weeks were not in evidence. They represented the Laurent family who had tried, and were still trying, to stop the film being made. Libel, they said. Joanna must have typed and dispatched more than two dozen letters on this tedious subject since shooting began, yet another chore for the dogsbody. Production Co-ordinator indeed!

Another of her duties, now occupying everybody's attention, was the delivery of each day's filming to the airport. At Marseille-Marignane she handed it over to their freight agent who dispatched it immediately, and under special arrangement with French and British Customs, to Technicolor in London, there to be processed and printed. On this 18th April the shipment included not only the film they had just shot but Mr Nelson (Zoom-Zoom) Rocca's final day's work with the principal actors.

Young Johnny sealed the precious cans and gave them to her. Suddenly there were more hasty kisses, more farewells. Old Tom was off to Ischia where his patient film-widow wife was waiting for him; his cameraman was flying back to London; the other two were driving the camera-truck across France, with many a bibulous stopover no doubt; it was already packed and prepared for departure.

''Bye, Jo—see you in ten days. See you at the studio. See you,' and they were gone, leaving Joanna and Marc Gérard, sole survivors of a unit which had at one time numbered a hundred and five people. As the camera-truck swung out of the parking-lot and down the hill, young Johnny shouted, 'Careful, Jo! Don't do anything I wouldn't do.' She knew what they were thinking, and it wasn't true. But all the same her stomach saw fit to turn over when Marc nodded goodbye to his type-cast mafioso friend and came towards her little car. Wide shoulders, slim hips, an open and friendly manner which she did not expect in a Frenchman. (They were, in her opinion, a lot of secretive and self-assured tom-cats.)

Not that Marc Gérard lacked the self-assurance, which came, she had been told, from a European tradition of strong family bonds and early inclusion into the adult structure. Whatever the reason, she found it attractive, calming; in her world too many people were always in the process of 'finding' themselves, or being 'born again', or whatever; it was nice to meet somebody who seemed to know who he was, and for whom one birth was sufficient.

He was a light brown young man: his hair, his tanned face, attractive and lively, even his eyes which sometimes had a strange golden glint in them. He came from country stock on both sides of the family; his father was a farmer in Normandy, his uncle had inherited the vineyard near Marseille. Marc's choice of a career, in which he had not so far been notably successful, amused them all: particularly because, between films, he chose to labour in the northern wheatfields or among the southern vines according to season and inclination.

He leaned into the car and regarded her perceptively, intently: a regard which had from the first been new to her, since the eyes of most American men were restless and always seemed to be looking around for something more interesting, more glamorous—more. Even Barney, who she was inclined to think had really loved her, was a slave to this habit. As usual she was fascinated and unsettled by Marc's all-embracing examination of her: and at his sudden proximity her stomach maddened her by turning over again. Thank God he was only employed for the location, to cope with French extras, crowds, police, traffic, and would not be reappearing in England where, it was to be hoped, her stomach would regain its equilibrium.

He said, 'Dinner tonight? For old times' sake.'

'No, Marc.'

He glanced at his watch. 'Lunch—it's one-thirty.' He spoke excellent English because, as a boy, he had often made the short journey from Normandy to Sussex, there to spend holidays with an aunt, his father's sister, who had married an Englishman. 'Lunch,' he added mockingly, 'is very safe.'

'I'm going to the airport.'

He nodded, eyeing her. 'If I had behaved badly I could perhaps understand it.'

'You understand darn well. *I* behaved . . . not badly, stupidly. I don't like casual things, I'm not made that way.'

'Of course. Why do you think I love you?'

Suddenly she felt tears rising up inside her; the fact enraged her so violently that anger triumphed over any other emotion. 'Please,' she said, 'we've played this scene. Go away.'

He straightened up and shrugged, looking young and vulnerable and hurt; this was unbearable, but more bearable than other ways of saying goodbye. She said, 'Marc, I'm sorry. Goodbye.'

'Au revoir, Jeanne.'

She drove away before either of them could speak again. Goodbye. Au revoir. Which was correct? Time would tell. Time was already, in its own circuitous way, beginning to tell as she accelerated out of the parking-lot and down the hill, right and then left into the Boulevard André Aune.

If only . . . 'If,' her mother occasionally said, 'is the most useless word in the language.' It simply had to be admitted, she was not like other girls, most of her friends in California, who could leap in and out of various beds as though on a trampoline. The thing to do with one's character was to meet it face to face, assess it as clearly as possible, and cooperate with it. All the same, as far as Marc was concerned, if only . . . Her mother, like her father, was a balanced academic of Danish ancestry; and anyway, balanced or not, there had in the past been blazing arguments over the aquavit and the vodka; both of them were passionate and multicoloured under the learned beige, but that was their problem and they coped with it admirably, efficiently.

She admired them but had difficulty in emulating them.

If she liked a man well enough to go to bed with him she was already half way to being in love with him; this was the burden she bore in a permissive age. And then there was ambition. She intended to make films. 'A Joanna Sorensen Production,' that was the goal. All right then, in lights, with a row of dazzling press quotes under the marquee. Best Film Of The Year, why not? It was high time the Best Film was also a good film; the two were not, as the cynics claimed, mutually exclusive.

Barney had mocked for a while, but he was no fool and had sized up the situation without rancour. 'You don't want me, you want an Oscar.' Crude, hurtful, and roughly true; she didn't necessarily want the Oscar but, by God, she wanted to make good films. You could count those already made on the fingers of one hand; or, to be charitable, two hands. 'You're hooked,' Barney had said before ambling away to his weekend wind-surfing and his snug job with Hughes Aircraft.

The thought of Barney Scott, old friend of two years, seemed to put into perspective Marc Gérard, casual lover of two weeks. Yes, it had taken her two whole weeks to break surface after that deep, deep plunge. Idiot!

At this point in her musing, satisfactory on the whole, there first entered her mind the idea that she was being followed: by a silver-grey Mercedes.

She had long since wended her way through lunch-time traffic to the Rue de Rome, along it, over the Canebière, up to the triumphal arch and so on to the autoroute leading to the airport or, some five hundred miles further on, to Paris. Had she noticed the Mercedes before? She wasn't sure, but vaguely thought that it might have stopped beside her at traffic-lights somewhere in the city. *Was* it in fact following her? She had been more concerned with her thoughts than with her driving, more concerned with the sick emptiness of parting from Marc than with the incidence of other vehicles; therefore she was not going fast and she was keeping to the slow lane. Many cars, both large and small, were continually passing her, so why not a powerful Mercedes SE 500 saloon, capable of at least 130 m.p.h.?

Immediately she thought of the Laurent family and their grey lawyers. 'Dear Monsieur Laurent,' her immediate boss, the Producer, had dictated. 'I have read your letter and taken note of the allegations contained in it, and I have notified my Studio accordingly. I understand that this whole matter was investigated and dismissed when the novel, upon which my film is based, was first published . . .'

'Dear Monsieur Laurent—I am under instruction from my legal advisers, both in Marseille and in Los Angeles, to ignore this correspondence which you have instigated, since it interferes with my work in producing a high-budget prestige motion-picture which is in no way based upon any incident concerning your family. In future, will you please address all communications to the said legal advisers here, Messieurs Roche et Santini, 276 Boulevard Longchamp . . .'

'Dear Monsieur Laurent—It can come as no surprise to you that I am returning your last letter unopened . . .'

As regards the Mercedes, vague suspicions were useless; what she required was proof. The thing to do, as learned from a myriad TV epics, was to slow right down to, say 25 m.p.h. She did so. The silver-grey Mercedes did the same. Not only were they following her, they didn't give a damn if she knew it: probably *wanted* her to know it. The time was now two p.m. Joanna Sorensen had started running.

3

She had no doubt that the Mercedes represented another facet of the Laurent family. Whether it contained one of the cinder-like lawyers or all three of them was beside the point; the point was that they had no interest in Joanna Sorensen personally, therefore they were interested in the film she was transporting. The more she thought about this, between St Antoine and the Aix-en-Provence turn-off, the more obvious it seemed.

She knew very little about the Laurents, but a great deal about the 'Fontaines' portrayed in the film, and it had always struck her as extraordinary that if there *was* any similarity, as Monsieur Louis Laurent claimed, he didn't keep quiet about it; for the Fontaines were a thoroughly unpleasant lot, sitting moreover on a thoroughly nasty secret, the sleeping dog of the title.

In the film, set in 1968 against the violent background of that benighted year—industrial mayhem, student rioting, barricades in the streets—this animal is not allowed to lie. A Fontaine grandson appears on a visit from the United States and begins to ask awkward questions about the death of his father at the end of World War II. The facts which his determination lays bare are harsh indeed.

The father had joined the Maquis, the French underground; had been captured by the Germans, tortured and imprisoned. And what should he find upon his liberation but that the rest of his family had enthusiastically collaborated with the Nazis, thus multiplying their already considerable fortune by ten. He was about to denounce them when they, in self-defence, killed him: the crux of the film being that his inquisitive son, by arousing the sleeping dog of the past, finds himself in danger of sharing the same fate.

Fair enough. Admittedly not the kind of story which Joanna Sorensen, Oscar-winning Producer, intended to make; but at least it was *about* something: love, greed, betrayal, fratricide, honour, revenge. But why on earth Monsieur Laurent, millionaire silk-merchant of Lyon, should lay claim to any affinity was beyond her. Marc, during those hectic and, literally, delirious two weeks, had explained it to her in terms which were so foreign to an American as to be meaningless. Apparently wartime collaboration with the old enemy was still a potent and destructive force in French life, particularly for a man with political aspirations, no matter that he had only been a teenager at the time of the incident in question. It seemed that Monsieur Laurent aspired politically.

In any case, whatever his reason, he had been moving heaven and earth for six weeks in order to prevent the film being made; and he had failed.

It did not seem to Joanna at all unreasonable that he should now resort to other tactics. By appropriating her two canisters of negative the lawyers would strike a mortal blow. The location unit had been disbanded; in certain cases, of which Marc was one, dispensed with. Loss of the film would mean that a new unit would have to be recruited and sent back to Marseille with the two stars, both charging astronomical overtime, and with three supporting actors; two of the latter would, by then, be working in another movie and a Broadway play respectively. Moreover, all this would have to be accomplished in July at the end of Studio shooting. Between April and July the South of France changes its whole visual character. In spite of Old Tom's magic camera, nothing would match properly. A key—no, *the* key—sequence would be ruined.

How much of this Monsieur Laurent, his family and his lawyers actually knew she could not tell; but their correspondence with her boss, the Producer, revealed that they had strategic sources of information. They must not, on any account, get their hands on those two reels of film.

It was with this decision firmly resolved that Joanna turned off the autoroute into the airport approach road: the usual ramification of intercrossing bridges, mystifying to some, but of no consequence to an American girl born and bred among the turnpikes of the East and the freeways of the West. In any case, she'd been making the journey almost every day for a month and a half. However, the thing that occurred as she completed the manœuvre and headed for

'Aéroport Marseille-Marignane' did indeed take her by surprise. There was a silver flash and suddenly the Mercedes was level with her; she caught a glimpse of men's faces, hard and purposeful, but even then the juddering impact as the side of the big car struck the side of her tiny Renault came as a complete shock.

They were barging her off the road. They were forcing her on to the downward ramp which would take her back to the autoroute, heading north. For a few seconds she wrestled with the steering-wheel, terrified, numb; and then merciful rage came to her rescue once again. No! By God, *no*! Who the hell did they think they were?

More or less without thought, other than her determination not to give in, she jammed on her brakes. The Renault slithered to a halt, half on the slow lane, half on the dusty roadside. Apparently this was unexpected; in a second the Mercedes was far ahead of her, also braking.

Only now did she glance in her rear-mirror, appalled by the thought that there might have been a gigantic truck immediately behind. Fortunately there were no vehicles of any sort immediately behind; they were all in the fast lane, and they were all angry with the driver of the Mercedes: a fine Southern display of horn-blowing, invective and insulting gestures; the big car swerved into the slow lane a hundred yards ahead of her, which meant that she couldn't drive on. Unless . . .

She glanced over her shoulder and saw that a gentlemanly taxi-driver in the fast lane had slowed down, enabling her to pull out ahead of him; this she did, in a spinning of wheels and a cloud of dust. The Mercedes, however (nobody likes large and expensive cars with badly-behaved drivers) was excluded from such *politesse*. Joanna accelerated past it, enclosed in a temporary convoy, and saw to her satisfaction that an overladen truck was emerging from factory gates, thus blocking her opponents' advance; the Mercedes was going to stay in the slow lane for several miles. First round, more by luck than good judgement, to Joanna Sorensen.

The adrenalin was pumping through her by now, generating a curious mixture of exhilaration and anger which she could not remember having experienced before; but she was too sensible a girl not to feel fear as well. As she approached the airport she thought of two things, indivisible. Firstly, that lustful ambition told her that if she lost the two canisters of film containing vital elements of a climactic sequence she would be held directly responsible, no matter what the circumstances, and Jack Kroll, Producer, would never forgive her.

Now Jack Kroll, an influential member of the movie Establishment, had been impressed by her efficiency and perhaps touched by her ambitions which exactly mirrored those of his own youth; he had promised her that on his next picture she should be Associate Producer: no great shakes as everybody knew, little more than a Production Co-ordinator in a different hat; but, professionally speaking, it would be a giant step off the secretarial ladder and on to the executive one. Joanna intended to take that step come hell or high water; therefore it was essential that she should dispatch the two reels of film and make sure that they reached London and Technicolor in safety.

At the same moment, intertwined with these thoughts, she saw in her mind's eye the dusty, often deserted strip of roadway to which the freight agents' offices were relegated. Monsieur Carlo César, whose company they were using, was in his own Southern way as efficient as she was: plump and jolly, always ready with a joke, always ready, unless she took evasive action, with a hug or even a pinch on the behind; she liked him very much, but was at this moment more aware of the fact that he was often not to be found, called away to supervise the loading of some important consignment. His office was then left in the care of a Bardot-like secretary whose other duties were obvious, and obviously paramount; sometimes it was locked.

In that forlorn and unfrequented part of the airport the remains of the Mistral would be whirling little eddies of dust; the men in the Mercedes could grab her film, violently if they felt like it, without attracting the least attention. As if to underline this uncomfortable scenario her rear-mirror now told her that the silver-grey monster had escaped incarceration in the slow lane and was separated from her by two vehicles only: the taxi with the gentlemanly driver and an airport bus.

The abrupt stop which had initially saved her had been a matter of pure luck, but it seemed that some adventurous and hitherto unsuspected aspect of her character, closely related to ambition no doubt, was a quick learner. She indicated that she was about to take the right-hand loop-road which led towards the freight area; in consequence the taxi and the bus passed her, their destination the terminal complex. Nothing now separated her from the Mercedes; naturally it too was indicating a right turn in order to follow her. Joanna began to edge into the loop-road, but then gave the little Renault full acceleration, swung back on to the main approach and headed for the airport itself. She saw with satisfaction that the less manœuvrable Mercedes had been tricked; had come to a stop; was reversing. It would catch up with her in seconds of course, but then seconds were all she needed in order to skid to an untidy halt in front of the terminal (No Parking), grab her shoulder-bag and the two canisters of film, and run into the building with its blessedly protective crowds of people.

Round Two to Joanna Sorensen? No, not exactly. Looking back, she saw that three men were jumping out of the Mercedes, leaving a fourth at the wheel. They ran in through the automatic doors and advanced upon her, purposefully.

On the instant the crowd all about her became neither blessed nor protective, merely a great many blind and preoccupied people going about their own business with anxious expressions; a sick sense of dread informed her that she could as easily be robbed in this mêlée, and with violence, as out there in the deserted cargo area. Her heart was pounding; her mouth had dried up and could have formed neither words nor a scream.

She backed against a British Airways information counter, empty, alas, and looked about her wildly. The three men stopped in front of her; they were not the grey lawyers; they were not wearing neat suits but casual clothes; they were altogether larger, rougher, more alarming. One said, 'If you please, mademoiselle—the film.'

She shook her head, still unable to speak.

'Give me the film, immediately. It means nothing to you —you are not conerned with it.'

This contempt (Not concerned! It was her whole future!) jerked her into speech: 'You can tell Monsieur Laurent to mind his own damn business.'

The man nodded; then, after an instant: 'Monsieur Laurent is used to getting his own way. You would be very foolish not to give me those containers.' He was advancing, eyes fixed on the two round cans clutched against her chest. They were black eyes of a curious dull opacity, without sparkle; he had grey hair cut short; he had very large and ugly hands. It was curious that she could remember nothing else about him, but even more curious that one of the other men should seem in some way familiar: not tall, thick-set, balding. This man was later to haunt her memory, but at the moment all that mattered was escape. She turned and bumped into a mother and three children, none of whom appeared to notice her; indeed it was as if everybody else in the large hall was moving in another dimension, another dream.

She had knocked one child flat; heard it wailing. She was running, away, anywhere, away from the men . . . and only then realized that she was in fact running towards the departure area: ticket-holders only, Immigration, and standing beside the Immigration Officer was . . . Oh God, an actual gendarme.

She reached him, gasping. He looked shocked; glanced at the canister, probably fearing some demented minority group with a bomb. She said, 'Please. Help me. I'm being followed, threatened. Those men . . .' She turned, pointing, but the men had naturally disappeared as if they had never, thirty seconds before, existed.

The gendarme looked politely beyond her. The mother had picked up her child and was soothing it while darting envenomed glances in Joanna's direction. Four Americans were approaching, passports at the ready; one of the women was saying, 'Yeah, sure it was a nice hotel, but it was a cat-house . . .'

The gendarme began to address Joanna in French, a language of which she properly understood perhaps twenty words. At this moment an extremely elegant young-old woman in Air France uniform, black hair swept back into a chignon, joined them; she gave Joanna a cool look and said, 'You speak French?'

'No.'

The woman turned on the gendarme with a flood of that awkward language; then said to Joanna, 'I tell him it is true; men were threatening you, I saw them. He asks why.'

'They wanted this film.'

The Air France lady looked at the top can and read the label. 'Ah, but yes, *Sleeping Dog*, we fly many of your personnel.' And this also she explained to the gendarme. Then: 'He says the film is finished here. He has read this two days ago in *Le Provençal*. I too have read it.'

Joanna explained her continuing presence in Marseille. The lady explained Joanna's explanation. 'The policeman asks if you wish a search for these men—if you wish to charge them with an offence.'

'No. I don't even know who they were.'

The lady smiled. 'Agents perhaps of Monsieur Louis Laurent.' The local papers had made hay out of that situation, as much as they knew of it, which was little. 'Come.

I think you should sit. Perhaps some coffee . . .' Ignoring Joanna's protestations with a professional's calm assurance —she must at one time have been a stewardess—she took the girl's arm and led her through an unmarked door. Joanna found herself behind the scenes of Air France; baggage was trundling by on a mechanical belt; other ground-staff were standing about off-duty. There were two 'toilettes' for staff use only. Her escort said, 'In here, perhaps. No one will find you.'

Sitting in her little cubicle, and sitting, later, with a cup of black coffee, she reviewed the odd situation in which she found herself and came to some reasonably calm conclusions. The important thing was the film; it must be delivered into the hands of Carlo César in person; once he had signed for it her responsibility was over, though she knew she wouldn't rest until he had reported that it was airbound for Heathrow.

Luckily, and for once, there was no hurry. Normally speed was of the essence, since the film was intended to reach Technicolor on the evening of its dispatch or first thing the following morning; it was then processed immediately; within an hour the Producer's representative had seen it, usually with the Editor. Both men reported back to the location on its quality and content, and, if there had been any mistakes or omissions, they suggested how these could be rectified. At the same time Technicolor were making a video of the footage in question, and this was sent straight back to Marseille where it could be seen and discussed by Director, Cameraman, Producer, etcetera. Normally. But the Producer was now in New York, the Director in Los Angeles, the Cameraman in Ischia; none would expect to see the results of the last two days' shooting for nearly a week. So there was no hurry.

But why, she wondered, her thoughts leaping off at a tangent, had that balding, thick-set man seemed familiar? Where had she seen him before, because she was quite sure that she *had* seen him before? Well, for God's sake, he was a local type, she must have passed a thousand variations of him in the street. Other things were more important.

What Mademoiselle Production Co-ordinator must now do was to give up any idea of shipping the film this afternoon; she must go to her hotel and telephone Technicolor, the Producer's London office, and the lawyers in Marseille, explaining that the family Laurent had once again tried to throw a spanner in the works but that the film was safe and would be dispatched within the next twenty-four hours.

Now, how was this to be achieved? Obviously she couldn't go back to her car, they'd be watching it. A taxi? No; if it came to another confrontation, how could a lone taxi-driver protect her from those bully boys? Of course, an airport bus! She knew exactly where they were parked: around a corner, out of sight of the terminal approach. So if the Mercedes was still where she'd last seen it . . .

Her brain was now functioning with its usual efficiency. She remembered that only a few yards from where she was drinking her coffee, on the other side of the unmarked door, was a gift-stall and bookshop; it also sold travel-bags. She said Goodbye and Thank-you to her Air France rescuer; said that all was well, she knew exactly what to do next.

It was not pleasant crossing to the gift-shop. Whereas she had at one time felt invisible she now felt that everybody was staring at her; but a sudden movement of passengers screened her movement, and she took refuge among the shelves of hideous souvenirs and racks of postcards without attracting any unwelcome attention.

Peeping, she could from this point ascertain that the silver-grey Mercedes was indeed still parked behind her Renault: an Avis rental which could be collected by them whenever she chose to telephone their office. She couldn't see whether all four men were sitting inside the car, but guessed that at least one would be posted in the hall, keeping an eye open for her.

She bought a travel-bag large enough to contain the film canisters; she bought newspaper with which to pad it out, thus blurring their distinctive shape; she bought a pair of dark glasses and put them on; she bought a dreadful plastic slide and fixed back her hair with it; she took off her windcheater, and thus, she hoped, marginally disguised, waited for another chattering group of people to emerge from the arrival gate. When they did so, she joined those who were headed for the waiting buses. She huddled among them to buy her ticket. She got on the bus, found an empty seat and sat as low as possible, the bag at her feet. Presently the driver climbed aboard, and they moved off. Only then did she dare to turn and look along the façade of the terminal, knowing that it would tell her a truth.

The truth was that the Mercedes was not following the bus, which could only mean that they hadn't seen her. She relaxed for the first time in one and a half hours—it was now three-thirty—and decided what she would do next.

It was not a difficult decision. The bus would deposit her in the middle of Marseille at the Gare St Charles, an impressive edifice approached by a flight of steps worthy of a palace or a Potemkin. Inside the railway station there would be a baggage-check; outside it, taxis were always waiting.

The Left Luggage office, when she found it, exceeded her most optimistic calculations; it was as secure as the average Bank and manned by a surly and suspicious band of minor French bureaucrats: than whom no soldier or policeman is more fearsome. She zipped the receipt into the innermost pocket of her shoulder-bag and left the station feeling buoyant, confident, a hundred pounds lighter, and—why not? —well-pleased with herself. No one knew that she had visited St Charles, no one had seen her deposit the bag, and the only evidence, a tiny slip of paper, was now securely hidden.

She got into the taxi, saying, '*Hôtel Pharo, s'il vous plaît, m'sieur,*' and the driver even understood her.

4

The Pharo had been chosen as unit headquarters because it was large and modern, and therefore supplied ample parking space for the attendant fleet of cars, vans, trucks. It stood on an eminence not far from Empress Eugénie's little palace of the same name and commanded the same view of the Old Port, crammed with yachts, and of the Mediterranean with, in foreground, Château d'If of stern repute.

The first thing Joanna saw, as her taxi swung into the hotel's forecourt, was the silver-grey Mercedes parked in front of the main entrance. The big man with the ugly hands and the matt black eyes was leaning against it, chatting idly to the doorman. Joanna gasped. At the same moment he turned, glancing towards the taxi, but by that time she had dropped sideways on to the seat. The sight of him had pricked the balloon of her buoyancy and banished her entire French vocabulary, all twenty words of it.

The driver was already slowing down, preparatory to pulling up in front of the door. She cried out, 'No, monsieur, please! Drive on, don't stop!' Then, '*Venez* . . . I mean, *allez!*' And, a triumph: '*Allez vite, vite!*'

'You are said Hôtel Pharo.' His English was peculiar, but better than her French; he was also, like all Marseillais, quick on the uptake; he had not stopped.

'Yes, but . . . Please, just drive on. I've . . . changed my mind.'

The driver glanced over his shoulder and took note of her position. Sexy girl: the explanation was probably some lover, ex-lover, whom she didn't want to see. He shrugged and drove around the forecourt, back into the Boulevard Livon.

Joanna did not raise herself. Her heart was again pounding violently. The seat smelled of dog, which she found oddly comforting. The man must have seen her, he *must*, or had she by the time he turned already flung herself down? The odd behaviour of the taxi must certainly have attracted his attention, conversation with the doorman can't have been that fascinating. Still semi-recumbent, she said, 'Monsieur, please . . . ? Are we . . . are we being followed?' After all she had compromised herself completely in his estimation; at the very least he must think her some kind of a nut, so what harm could the question do?

He glanced in his rear-mirror. 'An autobus and *les flics*. You wanted by police, uh?'

'Oh no! No.' But it had been a joke, and he at least found it amusing.

Joanna raised herself and took a furtive look behind them; the Mercedes was not in sight. Luck, so far, had been suspiciously benevolent; all the more reason to suspect that it would presently forsake her altogether. As if to emphasize this thought the driver now said, '*Alors*—where you go?'

They were bowling along the Quai Rive Neuve on the eastern side of the Old Port. Joanna had no idea where she wanted to go, but the sight of all those immaculate yachts in the brilliant sunshine, wind-meters tinkling and glittering at their mastheads, caused an immediate reaction in that other, more decisive, more adventurous Joanna who had behaved with such dispatch at the airport. It was this Joanna, rather than her timid twin, who said, 'Do you know a bar on the other side of the port, Bar des Moulins?'

A somewhat surprised eye examined her in the rear-mirror. '*Bien sûr.*'

She knew that the Bar des Moulins was not a place frequented by visitors; it was at the far end of the Quai du Port, away from the centre of the city and the more sophisticated cafés, nearer to the grim fortress of St Jean. It was popular with locals, and not with the more respectable locals at that. Adventurous and decisive Joanna seemed

well-pleased with her choice; timid and reasoning Joanna
was not. She had been introduced to the Bar des Moulins
by Marc Gérard.

This was why, as soon as she entered the battered, fuggy
bar (which was for some reason full—at four forty-five on
a Wednesday afternoon, the ways of the French were truly
incalculable) Madame Argenti of the brassy voice and rough
friendliness said, 'Alas, Marc is not here.' She said it in
French, but Joanna understood her perfectly, as did the
twenty or so men in the place, for Madame's voice could be
heard in every corner of her establishment and doubtless
far beyond.

Joanna felt compelled to say, quietly, with gestures, '*Marc
et moi*—' a finger to her chest—'*finis.*'

'Ah-hah!' Madame's black eyes glittered under her
tangled reddish curls. She was wearing a dress featuring
purple daisies and orange sunflowers. Her bosom and her
fine arms showed, more clearly than her collapsing features,
that she had once been an attractive woman; so did the
attitude towards her of the more elderly clients.

Eight of these at two tables were playing what appeared
to be some local variation of gin-rummy. Younger men were
battering to death two pin-ball machines. Bar football was
in rowdy mid-match beyond. Whereas in the past American
Joanna had found the place noisy, shabby, and in all respects
unhygienic, in her present circumstances she found it warm,
friendly, protective. It would be a foolhardy villain, however
large his hands, who dared to lay a finger on her here. One
word from Madame, and all these ebullient dogs, young
and old, would be at his throat.

She sat at the end of the counter and ordered coffee, aware
of the all-male scrutiny to which she was being subjected.
Women were rare in the Bar des Moulins, named, Marc
had told her, after the windmills which had once stood on
the hill behind it. Hideous blocks of flats had long since
taken their place.

Madame Argenti returned with the coffee, and a cognac which she explained was on her. So those black experienced eyes had looked right through the smooth young face to the turmoil within. She was, Joanna knew, some distant relative of Marc's. Occasionally he would go sailing with her large son, Jean-Michel, a dedicated Rugby-football player who part-owned one of those glittering yachts. Marc called him '*mon cousin*'; the unit had joked that everyone in Marseille was a 'cousin' to Marc . . . Hell to Marc!, she didn't want to think about him. But as this idea entered her head it held open the door for another, more subtle: had that bold Joanna already accepted certain hard facts which the timid twin was too reasonable even to consider? She was in trouble, how great a trouble she could not as yet know; she was alone in a foreign city, not understanding its ways and not speaking its language. Wasn't it possible, even downright likely, that she had come to this café because there was only one person in the whole of Marseille whom she could trust, to whom she could turn for help?

She put her elbows on the counter, her head in both hands, and considered this idea with the utmost unwilling-ness. She couldn't go back to the hotel, the very idea caressed her spine with icy fingers. She remembered again the crash of metal on metal as the Mercedes had tried to force her tiny Renault off the road. She heard the hard, accented voice: 'Give me the film, immediately.' The black unliving eyes looked at her again with . . . with nothing, that was what had been frightening about them, about the man. To him she was nothing: a nothing which stood in his way.

Quite suddenly, shock, long delayed, crept up on her and made her tremble. Determined that Madame should not mistake her emotion as relating to Marc, she seized the cognac and downed it. Fire kindled in her stomach, empty, she now remembered, since breakfast at seven o'clock.

She could not go back to the hotel, so how could she

make those all-important telephone calls: to London, to the lawyers here in Marseille, to New York?

Her father, knowing his rebellious child, had said to her more than once, 'Acceptance, you know, is half the battle; saves an awful lot of wear and tear. Always accept what you must.'

His daughter sighed her acceptance; its opposite seemed of a sudden to have been a mere token anyway, a formality. She said to bright-eyed Madame behind the bar, '*Moi, téléphoner. Téléphoner Marc.*' She didn't even resent Madame's evident approval. Young men existed to help attractive girls in trouble, wasn't that one of the more obvious facts of life?

TWO: TWO-SHOT—JOANNA AND MARC

1

He sat at the table, leaning forward, gold-flecked eyes fixed on her face, and listened. He had shown no surprise, and also no pleasure, at being called back from the limbo of 'Goodbye', but then he himself had merely said, 'Au revoir'. Also he was a Frenchman. Where, she wondered, did they learn this social/sexual tact? Why didn't men of other nationalities possess it?

When she had finished her story he nodded and began to make rings with his beer glass on the table, a corner table beyond the card-players where no one could hear them. She thought, not for the first time, that when it was fore-shortened as now, and when the intelligent eyes were hidden, his face changed its entire character, becoming tough, powerful and, as he so often said of himself, peasant.

He nodded decisively, looked up at her and said, 'First the lawyers. What's the number?'

She gave it to him. He retired to the telephone at the end of the bar and hunched himself over it, a typical young Frenchman in corduroy jeans and leather jacket. After a couple of minutes he came back to her and said, 'They don't seem surprised, they think Laurent's capable of anything. Roche says he'll try to find out what's going on, who those men are. Your description of the car will help. He'll call me back at my apartment.' Then he smiled and picked up her hand. 'Don't look so frightened.'

'I am frightened.'

'No need. Where's the ticket—for the film, the travel-bag?'

'Safe in here.'

'Okay, let's go to the Pharo. From your room you can call London and New York. Yes?'

She wondered, not for the first time, what in hell the women's libbers were actually talking about, relieved that at least she didn't have that problem to inhibit her. A man's presence was reassuring, why quibble about anything so obvious?

She said 'au revoir' and thanks to Madame Argenti, who gave her a curt nod, as much as to say, 'Good girl! I always knew you had your head screwed on properly.' A certain amount of omniscient smiling and eye-catching would follow their exit, but were not displayed in her presence.

Marc's Fiat was parked on the pavement where, later in the year, Madame would deploy tables and chairs and a few faded sunshades. This illegal parking, widespread all over the city, had at first surprised Joanna, but now she was used to it. Just let him try parking on the sidewalk in Los Angeles!

Driving back around the Old Port, he said, 'I'm pleased that you called me.' The personal note must have caused some emanation from her jangled nerves, for he added quickly, 'It would have been foolish not to, and you are not foolish.'

As they approached the Hôtel Pharo she was unable to stop her hands gripping the seat on either side of her body. He glanced at them but said nothing.

The silver Mercedes was no longer in evidence. Marc looked at her face. 'No?'

'No. But that doesn't mean . . .'

'Take it easy. We go carefully—I am not foolish either.'

There were parking spaces for perhaps twenty cars in front of the hotel; all were occupied. Joanna was glad that he didn't drive down into the main parking area underneath the building, cavernous and dark. Instead, with true local swagger, he bumped up into the kerb, straddling double

yellow lines. He said, 'Keep your eyes open. If you see one
of them . . .'

She nodded; and again that swarthy face which, at the
airport, she had known but not known flashed into her
memory, and disappeared.

The vast lobby was almost deserted: calm and quiet. A
few people were taking tea and gazing out at the Château
d'If; waves were breaking over the harsh rocks, leaping and
sparkling; the Mistral might have withdrawn, but it had not
yet settled into its summer slumber. Joanna collected her
key. Marc said, 'Have there been any inquiries for
Mademoiselle?' No, none.

In the elevator he looked at her, smiling his open smile
which was seldom as ingenuous as it seemed. 'You must get
in trouble more often, it suits you.'

She was touched, knowing that the flattery was largely
intended to soothe her nerves, surprised to find that in a
way it did so; but inwardly she recoiled from this intimacy,
and he, recognizing the withdrawal, shrugged but continued
to smile. She had of course realized that calling upon him
for help would produce its crop of personal difficulties, how
could it not? Therefore she kept her mind fixed on the
practical problems which faced her, most imminently two
complicated long-distance telephone calls; so that he was
still smiling and she was frowning in concentration when
she unlocked the door of Room 377. Revealing chaos.

The bed had been turned over, the mattress slit and the
underlining torn off the base. All drawers had been opened
and emptied, also the hanging cupboards, and her two
suitcases thrown, yawning, on top of her clothes; most
shocking of all, her papers were scattered like a snowstorm
overall. She moved forward, crying out in sick anger, but
Marc thrust her back against the door and said, 'Stay there!'

Only when he had looked into the bathroom and the
closets did he turn to her, hands spread, face grim.

'But *why*?' she cried, too disgusted to move from the door.

'They're not interested in me, they want the film.'

Marc came over to her, picked up a chair and sat her down on it; after closing the door, he said, 'That may have been true this afternoon. Now it's no longer true.'

Joanna nodded, her wits regrouping themselves. She had given them the slip at the airport, and they knew that she would no longer be carrying the film about with her. Somewhere there'd be evidence as to where she had put it. Why not in this room?

Marc said, 'You see?'

She nodded again, but she had not seen it all, and did not do so until he added, 'You're in danger, Jeanne, you're the only person who can tell them where to find it.'

Her stomach fell away as it was inclined to do in express elevators or on roller-coasters. 'Not the only person—I told *you*.'

'They may not know we've met. I hope not.' He went to the window and looked out over the entrance to the port and the two fortresses, originally placed there by Louis XIV to remind his mother's unruly ancestors that Marseille was part of France. He said, 'This is perhaps why that man was waiting outside with the Mercedes—keeping watch while the others . . . did this.'

She thought that it might also explain why he hadn't followed the taxi even if, as she suspected, he had seen her in it.

Marc turned back. 'You can't stay here, you must come to my place—and nobody must see you do it. With any luck . . .' He didn't continue. Earlier, she had suspected that Luck had been overindulgent towards her and that this state of affairs was unlikely to continue; the same thought had evidently crossed his mind.

Up to the moment of opening the door of the hotel room neither of them had perhaps treated the matter all that seriously. Joanna had been protecting the two reels of film because of a mixture of anger, duty and personal affront, and because its disappearance would undercut her considerable ambition; Marc had understood because he too was a professional and could appreciate the technical difficulties this disappearance would cause; more personally, he was pleased that she had recalled him from limbo, thus re-establishing some of the old intimacy. But this carnage posed a new threat of a different kind; violent men were at large, prepared to use further violence. How far would that violence go? What would such men be prepared to do in order to get what they wanted? Hesitantly Marc said, 'Jeanne, it would perhaps be . . . sensible to let them *have* the film.'

'No!' Facing the brilliant sky outside the window, the grey eyes flashed with blue sparks of defiance. He wondered why obstinacy, which made so many women look ugly, made this one look beautiful. 'Okay, let's move—I don't like it here.'

'But I *must* call New York and London.'

'From my apartment.' He glanced around at the disorder. 'We will find and pack what you need, only what you need.'

'The management ought . . .'

'Hell to the management! They can clear up the mess later. We don't want them here now, calling the police, all that. Yes?'

'Yes.' She was surprised by this terse, perhaps ruthless aspect of him. But why? Only half an hour ago, in the bar, she had seen it so clearly in his features; also he had been a first-class Second Assistant, helping the Production Manager surmount every kind of awkward obstacle, commanding crowds of excitable extras who obeyed him implicitly: no mean feat if one considered that they were Marseillais.

Something was still worrying him; he said, 'Jeanne, I think you should give me the ticket, the receipt for that travel-bag. As far as we know, they are not looking for me. And they will find it more difficult to . . . take it from me by force.'

She extracted it from the shoulder-bag and gave it to him
without question; mistrust had never been numbered among
the things which divided them. He took the little white slip
of paper, and then stood for quite a long time, staring at it,
frowning, far away in thought.

'What's the matter?'

'Nothing.' The light brown eyes came up to hers. Their
colour, even the occasional golden glint in them, had always
reminded her of a retriever possessed by her parents when
she was a child, a gentle animal like all its breed. She now
realized that Marc's eyes, unlike those of the dog, could
become hard, secretive, even dangerous, but only much
later would she understand that the realization had been in
the nature of a warning.

He pulled a wallet from the inside pocket of his leather
windcheater, put the ticket into it, replaced the wallet and
buttoned the pocket. 'Now . . .' He indicated the chaos
around them. 'Only what you need, we can collect the rest
later.'

The job was not as difficult as the look of the place
implied; Joanna was used to locations and took no unnecessary clothing; her paperwork, which seemed to cover the
whole room, could be contained inside one large document
case. While she was collecting the necessities and packing
them, Marc said, 'You must change too. If they're looking
for you they'll expect a girl dressed as you are now. Put on
something—' with a grin—'feminine.'

During this transformation he sat on the wreckage of the
bed, again lost in his own thoughts. She guessed that he
would not voice them because in his estimation she had
taken enough punishment for the time being: with the
prospect of more to come. She couldn't know, any more
than he could, that if at this moment he had brought himself
to tell her the truth it would have saved a great deal of
disastrous misunderstanding.

When she was dressed he abandoned cogitation and

smiled. 'Very pretty. I prefer you as a woman.' Then, again
serious: 'We must not leave together, we must not be seen
together. Here is what we do.'

2

The plan started with Joanna departing from the hotel by
taxi: without her suitcase, needless to say; he would take
that and the document case in his car. Her destination was
Métro Castellane.

She had never used the Marseille Métro before and was,
in her present state, quite sure that something would go
wrong. It did, starting as soon as she had entered the
station and brought a ticket. There were automatic turnstiles
standing solidly mute between her and the trains. She inserted the ticket into the requisite slot; it popped out as
expected but the gate would not open. She tried again. And
again, panic rising. A train rumbled in and came to a
stop. God in heaven, if they were following her they'd be
immediately behind her right now; and right now, as she
tried the accursed ticket yet again, she saw that there was
indeed a man immediately behind her. Moreover, he was
observing her strangely, hiding a kind of canny interest.

He was slim, wiry, Italianate. When he reached forward
and took the ticket out of her hand she nearly screamed. He
turned it over and inserted it into the slot; the gate opened.

By now the train had rumbled away and the platform
was deserted: just the two of them. Again she was aware of
his eyes on her. When the train arrived he entered the same
compartment; knowing that he continued to watch, she
could *not* keep her eyes from straying towards him. Luckily
there were four other people sitting between them.

She didn't even notice the first stop, something to do with
Paradise. At Vieux Port three more passengers joined them.
The watcher kept darting glances in her direction; he had
a somewhat brutal profile; could he have been the third man

at the airport? No mental picture of that faceless individual presented itself.

At Colbert all seven of her companions got out, leaving them alone together. Quite how she lived through the short journey to St Charles she would never know; she made up her mind to change compartments as soon as they got there. However, railway stations are all the same; some thirty people filled the carriage with noise and laughter. Not that this stopped the man watching her, but at least occasional bodies hid her from his view, giving her momentary relief, allowing her brain to function. Marc had told her to get off at Cinq Avenues, Longchamp where he would be waiting for her. There was now only one stop, Réformes, before they arrived there. If the man didn't get off at Réformes, ought she to sit tight and go past the meeting-place? If she did, Marc would think that something dire had befallen her; if she didn't something dire might befall them both, and in any case they'd certainly be seen together.

Réformes. The man did not get off. Marc had said that after Cinq Avenues the suburbs began; that meant fewer and fewer people; violent occurrences on underground railways always happened in the suburbs. Yet how orderly, clean, smooth it all was: utterly unlike the clanking, lurching pandemonium of the New York Subway or London's dreary, dirty Underground. Surely nothing ugly could occur on this trim little train? Oh yes it could!

In the end, unable to bear the tension any more, and taking a six to one chance (if he wasn't tailing her, there were another five stations to the end of the line) she alighted at the Five Avenues as arranged. And, oh God, so did the man!

Her floundering wits told her that she must let him get ahead of her; in this way, somehow, she might be able to warn Marc to stay clear. She passed through the ticket-barrier and found a map of the city's public transport system. She studied it closely. Out of the corner of her eye she could see that the man had not gone ahead of her and now . . . *now he was coming towards her!*

Everybody else had left the station, no one in sight. He was beside her. The thin, malignant face was scarred along the jaw-bone. What was he carrying inside that rolled newspaper? A knife? A hypodermic?

'Mademoiselle needs help?' And, receiving no reply: 'Mademoiselle would do me the honour of taking a café, a glass of wine?'

Minutes, hours perhaps, passed before she understood that it was nothing but a pick-up, a clumsy attempted pick-up, something which had happened to her a hundred times. Relief made her feel so faint that she was afraid she might drop at his feet. She managed to say, '*Non, merci, monsieur.*'

'But there is . . .'

'*No!*' She had not meant to scream at him but her nerves chose this moment to break. He paled under the olive skin as if the Mistral had hit him, turned and hurried up the steps out of her life.

When she thought her legs would perform the necessary actions she followed, mounted into daylight and saw, opposite the station, Marc in his Fiat, looking anxious.

This experience had taken her mind off the moment when she would have to re-enter his apartment, though it was not in fact his but had been lent to him for the duration of filming by yet another 'cousin'. She supposed that there was really very little of Marc in it and yet, for her, the place was redolent of him and of their love-making. In order to hide her emotion she went to the window and looked out; for she was moved almost to tears by a sudden flood of happy memories, and happiness now seemed so distant, so ordinarily blessed. Worse, she could not at this moment think why on earth she had ever turned her back on him. If he had taken her in his arms right now and pulled her on to the bed she would not have put up even a token resistance.

The realization shocked her. Could so much actually have changed between them in . . .? It was only two hours since he had joined her at the Bar des Moulins. So she gazed out at the plane-trees, which had burst into pale green leaf since last she'd seen them, subdued these feelings, and was able, eventually, to turn and face him.

He was pulling the cork from a bottle of wine: one of his uncle's rosés, unlike any other she had ever tasted. Memories and emotion hit her again. He glanced at her, read her expression, and said, 'Drink this while I make an omelette, you're starving.'

'Marc, I should try those calls.'

'Leave them. You're too tired, you'll make no sense. In the morning.'

She accepted this curt advice thankfully. She sat on the bed, drank the wine, watched him, told him about her absurd experience on the Métro. It made them both laugh, and laughter drew them close together again, easily and naturally. Looking about her at well-remembered things, she could not believe that she had ever walked out of this room swearing never to return, *not* returning for three endless weeks. Now it was as if she had never left it, and she supposed that in a sense she never had. 'Acceptance is half the battle,' said her father's quiet, meditative voice. 'Saves a lot of wear and tear. Always accept what you must.'

She could easily accept that she had, to some degree or other, fallen in love with the young man now intent on his omelette; otherwise, being the anachronism she was, she would never have gone to bed with him. Yet herein lay a conundrum, because it was her very acceptance which had *made* her walk out: impossible situation, different nationalities, entirely different ambitions: she wanted to make good films; he, for God's sake, wanted to make a family! What would her father have to say about that one?

By the time they had finished eating, a deep blue twilight had fallen; then, suddenly, it was night. They were silent.

He took her hand and said, 'Tomorrow, while you are telephoning, I'll go to St Charles, get the film, take it to Carlo at the airport. Then you will be free for nine days, where will you go?'

Joanna didn't reply, so he continued: 'My uncle's *bastide* is big, he and my aunt love to entertain. There is little to do in the vineyard at this time of year. We could drive up into the hills and sit in the forests and watch the deer, and come back tired and drink very much of this good wine.'

She had no idea what she would have replied if at that moment the entry-phone had not emitted its angry little buzz. Marc sighed, shrugged, stood up and lifted it from its hook. She could hear the voice on the other end quite clearly: 'Monsieur Gérard? Monsieur Marc Gérard?'

'Yes.'

'Police.'

3

It seemed to Joanna that the nightmare could not possibly have become more entangled, yet here it was tying itself in unimaginable knots before her eyes.

The police were represented by a plain-clothes detective of some sort and two uniformed henchmen. The detective was tall, bony, a pronounced widow's peak seeming to cleave his long, yellowish face. The others were typical of the solid (usually Corsican, she had been told) gendarmes who stood about on street corners, wearing that odd expression common to policemen worldwide, bored wariness. At the moment they were meeting nobody's eye, listening attentively no doubt while studying walls and ceiling.

At first, and naturally, she had assumed that the visit would be concerned with her wrecked room at the Hôtel Pharo, but this assumption was far from correct. The plain-clothes man said, 'Monsieur Gérard, you are I think acquainted with a certain Jean-Michel Argenti, whose mother owns a Bar on the Quai du Port.'

'He's my cousin.'

'You share a yacht with him?'

'No. He shares a yacht with two friends. Sometimes I sail with them when I'm in Marseille.'

'Last year Jean-Michel Argenti was involved in a serious case. Drugs. Am I correct?'

'He wasn't "involved". He saw a package floating in the bay—he picked it up—it proved to contain heroin. He immediately handed it over to the police.'

Joanna realized that her understanding of the language had outstripped her ability to speak it; she understood enough of this to be amazed and mystified. Big, awkward Jean-Michel who played Rugby football at weekends!

'Monsieur Gérard, were you with him at the time?'

'No.'

'But you were in Marseille.'

'Yes.'

'It is our opinion that if things had gone to plan, Jean-Michel Argenti would have passed this package to you for disposal. Profitable disposal.'

'Not true.'

The detective looked at Joanna. 'Mademoiselle, have you . . .?'

'I don't speak French.'

He switched to careful but laboured English: 'How long have you known this man, Marc Gérard?'

'Seven, nearly eight weeks.' They had met before shooting began: pre-production.

'You are, forgive me, his mistress?'

She looked at Marc, who shrugged. 'We're . . . very fond of each other, yes.'

'It has been your duty to take to the airport, Marignane, boxes . . . How do you say it? Metal boxes containing film.'

'Yes.'

'Every day?'

'More or less every day.'

'For speed, these boxes are sent by special arrangement.'

'Yes.'

'They are not examined by Customs.'

'No, it would expose the negative. That's all negotiated beforehand.'

'Did you know that in certain of these boxes were hidden packages of heroin?'

'That's absolutely impossible.'

'Impossible, uh? Mademoiselle, were you today followed to the airport by men who threatened you?'

His knowledge was a shock, but many people had witnessed the incident, notably the chic lady from Air France and the gendarme himself. 'Yes, I was.'

'Do you know who these men were?'

'I think they're employed by Monsieur Louis Laurent, whose lawyers . . .'

'Does it not seem possible to you that they were members of the underworld involved in the traffic of drugs, trying to seize the consignment you were carrying?'

She realized that it did indeed seem possible: the look of them, their whole manner. She nodded.

'You did not, I think, deliver the boxes to your agent, a Monsieur César.'

'No, I didn't.'

'Therefore you, and you—' a bleak glance at Marc—'will understand that we believe them to be hidden here in this apartment.'

Marc snorted derision. 'There's no film in my apartment, certainly no drugs. I suppose you've got a search warrant?'

'Certainly.' He produced the document in question and held it out under the younger man's nose.

Joanna, who had been fighting with her stampeding thoughts, now managed to pull them to a standstill. Obviously the whole thing was a ridiculous mistake; Marc would never get mixed up in such misdemeanours: not only was he too decent, he was far too intelligent. And yet this way of using the automatic Customs clearance of film was nothing if not intelligent. No, no, it was a preposterous allegation. Marc of all people!

He had moved to her side. 'It's all utter nonsense, I don't have to tell you that.'

'*Did* Jean-Michel pick up the package?'

'Yes. Last July. He took it to the police at once. The bay is a famous dropping-point, merchant ships, you must have heard about it.'

'If you please, Monsieur, Mademoiselle, I prefer that you remain silent.' He and his men were now dissecting the little apartment, no more than a single room with kitchen-extension and bathroom, what the French call a *studio*. They worked expertly and methodically. Since the objects they were looking for were comparatively large there were few places where they might be hidden.

Having recovered from the initial shock, Joanna's thoughts now returned to what the policeman had said regarding the men in the Mercedes. There was no doubt that his suggestion made complete sense of everything they had done: trying to force her off the road, intimidating her inside the terminal, tearing apart her hotel room. That kind of behaviour accorded much better with crooks, and she had seen all the movies, than with Monsieur Laurent and his lawyers and their desire to stop a film being made.

And when you came to think about it, how easy it would be for somebody, not Marc naturally, to get to . . . for the sake of argument, say young Johnny, junior member of the camera-crew; how easy for him to seal a package into the canister with the film, it was one of his duties to see to that. He was a pleasant and seemingly honest boy, but the vast profits of the drug-trade had perverted many a pleasant and honest boy before now . . .

Oh, for heaven's sake! What was the matter with her? It

made no sense whatever. The fact of the matter was that her brain was reeling about, punch-drunk after the twelve-round contest of this interminable day. (If anyone had told her that the complications were only just beginning she would not have believed them.)

The policemen had now finished their search; obviously they had found nothing. How could they find anything when what they sought reposed in the Gare St Charles? For an instant, in her weariness, she considered telling them the whole story, thus forcing Marc to surrender the ticket. Luckily she held her tongue.

The detective now crossed to the window and picked up her shoulder-bag which she had balanced on the sill. 'I apologize, Mademoiselle, this is necessary.'

As she watched him take out her belongings one by one and place them on the table among the remains of their meal, she could think of only one thing: Marc's wallet, buttoned into the inside pocket of his windcheater which was now lying on the bed. She glanced at him, and was surprised to find that he had changed entirely during the minute or so since last she had looked at him; from a kind of dull, dogged rage his expression had become canny and sharp. Why?

The plain-clothes man forestalled further self-question by saying, 'You, Monsieur, I'm sure you have a wallet.'

Marc picked up the jacket, extracted the leather folder and handed it over without protest, but still with that calculating expression on his face. The detective opened it and began to remove cards and photographs with care, examining each. Realization that the baggage receipt was no longer there struck Joanna at exactly the moment that Marc performed what was to her the most extraordinary action of this extraordinary day: he turned and picked up the telephone which was only a couple of feet from him on the bedside table. The policeman turned sharply. 'Put that down, Monsieur Gérard, what do you think you're doing?'

In English Marc replied, 'Calling the police, of course.'

If there had been any sanity or order in the situation up to this point, it now flew out of the window. All three policemen moved as one. The plain-clothes officer took three paces forward, nearly upsetting the table, and delivered some kind of karate-chop which knocked the receiver flying; at the same time one of the gendarmes flung himself at Marc, who raised a knee sharply but missed the man's groin. Joanna found herself seized by the second gendarme whose body momentarily obscured the rest of the room; her struggle lasted no more than a few seconds, partly because he was extremely strong and partly because her law-abiding mind whispered something about resisting arrest.

When she could see things clearly again, Marc's opponent had incapacitated him with a paralysing half-nelson. Marc tried to stamp on the man's foot, but a little more pressure brought him to his knees, gasping.

The detective issued a sharp order. Joanna found herself lifted across the room and thrust into the tiny bathroom. A moment later Marc was hurled past her; his body knocked her on to the bidet, while he tripped over her feet and crashed into the shower, bringing down curtains and rails. The door was slammed upon them. It could not be locked from outside, but a rattling of the handle indicated that some kind of fastening was being swiftly improvised. By the time they were able to disentangle themselves and regain their feet they had been imprisoned.

The events of the last three minutes were now sorting themselves out in Joanna's mind; she gazed at him in astonishment. 'They're . . . not the police.'

'No.' He shook his head as if to see whether it was still on his neck; clearly there had been blows during the seconds when the man had stood between herself and the room; his left eyebrow was contused and bleeding. Angrily he said, 'What a fool! Why didn't I see it at once?'

'I don't know how you saw it at all—he had a search warrant.'

'I imagine you can pick them up for a song if you know the right people.' He held up a hand and they were both silent; no sound now from behind the door. Then the unmistakable whine of the elevator descending. 'The search warrant was for the apartment, for my possessions. If they wanted to search your bag they should have taken you to the police station, done it in front of a witness, listing each article—every policeman knows that.'

'Where's the receipt?'

'Thank God I've got *some* sense. I hid it in the salt-box when I was making our omelette.'

The door had been tied shut with a length of nylon cord. With the weight of both their bodies they were eventually able to stretch this, to force the door open a crack, and to wedge it open with the handle of a toothbrush. Through the slit Marc could just manage to manipulate a razor-blade and sever the cord. The living-room, when they regained it, looked surprisingly unravaged considering the struggles which it had so recently witnessed; indeed it seemed to view their dishevelment with some surprise.

While she was seeing to the wound above his eye, Joanna said, 'Marc, who were they?'

'Monsieur Laurent's gone mad—evidently.'

'You don't think . . .? Could there be something in what he said? Those guys in the Mercedes weren't Monsieur Laurent's style at all. More like . . . really, gangsters.'

He nodded, thinking his own thoughts again, eyes hidden from her.

'Are you sure Jean-Michel isn't into heroin?'

'You're joking! That was just their excuse to search the place.'

'I guess so.'

'Jeanne, you know Michel, he's as open as a *crêpe*. He was terrified when he realized what he'd picked up, he *ran* to the nearest Gendarmerie—it's still a joke in the bar.'

For some reason she couldn't define, bat-like doubts continued to flit about in the shadows of her mind: too many odd things had happened, none of the pieces in the puzzle fitted together. 'I wonder why the lawyers never called you back?' Perhaps Messieurs Roche et Santini were not what they seemed to be either.

Her question had made them both glance at the telephone; both of them remembered how expertly and savagely it had been struck out of his hand. Their eyes met. He said, 'We're crazy, what are we doing sitting here? If they come back . . .'

No need to elaborate. Pursuit and intimidation had failed, trickery had failed; whoever 'they' were, the mask would now be dropped, the knives would be out.

Until this moment Joanna had not properly realized how much, how very much, she wanted to lie down on the bed and to feel his arms around her, to make gentle love, and then to sink into deep and blessed sleep. But of course he was right. 'Where can we go?'

He pondered the matter in silence, doubtless considering various relatives and discarding them for various reasons. 'A cheap hotel would be safest—just for one night.'

So, once again, they packed what they needed and set forth upon what, in Joanna's mind, was beginning to feel like a journey without end. An hour later they fell into a large, perhaps slightly damp, bed at the Hôtel Métropole-St Charles, one of many hostelries both more and less salubrious clustered about the railway station. It smelt powerfully of cats and drains.

Only then, and at last, were they able to lie in each other's arms; it seemed to both of them more like three years than three weeks since they had last made love. Later, encircled by his warmth, she said, 'Marc, you *will* take the film to the airport, first thing tomorrow?'

'Of course.' He stroked her hair gently, pleased to feel how their love-making had drawn all the tension out of the slim body. 'First we will ring the lawyers, arrange for you to go to their office. You can call London and New York from there. Meanwhile I'll go to Marignane and explain things to Carlo. He'll put the film on the first plane to Heathrow, you know him. It will reach Technicolor by lunch-time. After that we can make decisions.'

She nodded like a child being told a comforting fairytale, and nuzzled into his shoulder. She wanted to tell him many things: how good he smelled, how happy she was to be with him again, close to him . . . but sleep suddenly whisked her away.

He lay awake for quite a long time, thinking, frowning at the cracked ceiling, listening to the gentle sounds of her sleep. She was exhausted—why not, she had been running for eleven hours? It was as well that neither of them could foresee the continuing marathon which lay ahead.

4

She awoke violently, still enmeshed in some terrifying but fast-fading nightmare. But the dream had not been as terrifying as the thought which immediately sprang into her mind, or had perhaps invaded it by stealth while she slept. She knew exactly where she had first seen the balding, thickset man who had seemed so familiar at the airport, and she knew why she had not recognized him there and then: because he had taken off the dark glasses which, before, had masked his features. She had seen him standing in the parking-lot at Notre-Dame-de-la-Garde when she had come down from the church, filming completed, *and he had been talking to Marc.*

She felt physically sick. She wanted to throw off the bare brown arm which rested lightly across her. The sound of his soft and steady breathing infuriated her beyond measure, as did the memory of their love-making. She had to force herself to lie motionless; will herself to consider the matter rationally; perhaps after all it had been part of the night-mare.

Part of the nightmare certainly, but not a sleeping one. She had seen Marc talking to that man not half an hour before realizing that the Mercedes, with the man inside it, was following her. Marc knew everyone in Marseille, or so it seemed; he was, the unit had joked, related to most of them; he was related to big Jean-Michel who had picked up a package of heroin out there in the bay, and there could be a hundred guilty reasons why Jean-Michel had seen fit, been forced by circumstance, to hand it over to the police . . .

No, no, that was ridiculous; there was no reasonable connection between the links of this chain which her imagination was forging. In the first place Marc was a friendly young man, easy with everyone; and his job for the past eight weeks had been to contact hundreds of people who could be of use in making a film: a number of them had probably been crooks, a number always were . . .

But his *attitude* to the man! On first seeing them she had not wondered what mafioso-like stranger was asking him idle questions but who his mafioso-type *friend* could be. And was it mere coincidence that Marc, related to Jean-Michel who had picked up heroin in the bay, had been talking to a man who, a few minutes later, was pursuing her in a fast car in order to lay hands on two canisters of film said by the phoney policeman to contain heroin? She didn't believe in coincidences like that . . .

But of course it *could* have been coincidence. The man could have deliberately approached an innocent Marc in order to extract certain information which Marc, in all innocence, might well have given him. Also, for God's sake, Marc was an efficient Second Assistant, not an experienced actor; his concentrated attention when she had first told him her story in the Bar des Moulins couldn't possibly have been assumed; nor his shock upon seeing her ransacked room; no, nor any of his subsequent actions, particularly those relating to the visit of the 'police'. Of course he was perfectly innocent . . .

But if he was innocent, why had he kept so many of his innermost thoughts hidden from her? Noticing this in her wrecked room at the Hôtel Pharo she had thought that he was doing so, quixotically, to save her further worry; but that needn't have been the true reason at all . . .

Suspicion in a general sense is a harmless complaint, easily cured by a mental aperient and some rest. Suspicion of a loved one belongs to a different genus; it bleeds internally and festers, and the only cure is a scalpel. Four hours later, by the time dawn crept with a grinding of traffic into the hideous room—plum-coloured Paisley wallpaper, yellow oak furniture circa 1935—Joanna's imagination had run riot and impelled her into a state bordering on mania.

Marc awoke soon afterwards; everyone in the film industry was accustomed to wake early. Of course the rational expedient would have been to demand an outright answer to her suspicions, but she was now far beyond rationality. She was unable to hide her mood from him, but could conceal its ugly genesis.

'What's the matter?'

'Nothing. I couldn't sleep.'

'Nerves—you were overtired. It'll be different tonight when everything's settled.'

Yes indeed, it would be very different when everything was settled. In her present state there was only one thing she could do, and she had already decided exactly how to do it. That decisive and quick-witted twin, who had come to her aid at the airport and at various moments thereafter, was now showing a different side to her nature, making sinuous and deceitful plans.

To escape from the cats and the drains they took their breakfast around the corner in a café on the Allées Gambetta. It would have been pleasant to sit outside it on this perfect Mediterranean spring morning, gulls floating against a sky of cloudless blue, but they dared not do so for fear of some unknown watcher who might recognize them. In any case Joanna's mood would have preferred rain and the angry Mistral.

Leaving her to coffee and croissants, Marc retired to telephone the lawyers; returned to say that they had received no reply from Monsieur Laurent's legal advisers apart from a stale old reaffirmation of the fact that they intended to stop the film being finished. 'Santini's pretty sure they're bluffing.'

'Bluffing, bluffing,' whispered the cunning voice into Joanna's ear, 'we'll see who's bluffing!' Why, come to that, should she believe any of this reported conversation? Even if she had listened to it she couldn't have understood a word, and well he knew it. And when, a few minutes later, he said he must ring Carlo César at the airport to warn of his impending arrival, why should she believe he was doing any such thing? He could as well be telephoning his thick-set, mafioso friend. She loathed herself for all these suspicions, so alien to her nature, but they had grasped her with their talons and she could not escape them; she was their prisoner.

Marc offered to guide her to the lawyers' office, but she said she had been there several times before, and the Boulevard Longchamp wasn't far away. They arranged to meet at this café at midday; he kissed her and told her to take care and not to show her face more than was necessary. He added that he wasn't going to use his car in case somebody recognized it. 'I'll take the airport bus like you did.'

They set off in opposite directions. As soon as he had disappeared around the corner into the Boulevard d'Athènes she turned swiftly and ran back in pursuit of him, her heart pounding, her mouth stiff and dry as if stuffed with deceit. She followed him up the wide thoroughfare, keeping well away in case he should turn and see her; he did not turn;

appeared to be lost in thought. Even now, spying on him like this, she was aware of the deep feeling which he aroused in her; this awareness made her dislike herself all the more, but did not deflect her purpose.

He began to climb the grandiose steps leading to the railway station. She followed at a distance. Arabs sat upon the steps as they always did, surrounded by strange pieces of luggage, sometimes by whole families. Waiting. For what? She had never known and never would, but didn't like the way they eyed her, nor the way some of them eyed her shoulder-bag which, in this area, she always held more tightly.

Marc reached the top of the steps, approached the station, was swallowed up by deep shadow. There was no need to follow him into the arcade which housed, among other things, the baggage-check; admittedly there were two exits, but she could observe both of them from the other side of the main concourse. One of the impressive high-speed trains was about to depart for Paris; it was easy to hide among assembling passengers.

Presently Marc emerged from the arcade carrying the travel-bag; he turned towards the main entrance, outside which the airport buses were waiting. Joanna, hurrying after him, was aware of a tiny, unexpected gleam of relief in the blackness which encased her, because, no doubt about it, he was heading for the front bus which would be the first to leave. The gleam widened like a sunrise; she had totally misjudged him; all her stupid suspicions had been . . . He walked straight past the bus and down the ramp leading away from the station.

Joanna found herself turned to stone, unable to move, lost once more in darkness. Proof that he was not, never had been, taking the film to the airport seemed to have knocked the life out of her. Apparently suspicion confirmed was the worst blow of all.

There was a car parked half way down the ramp. Perhaps

it was a taxi; perhaps he had after all decided against the
bus.

No, it wasn't a taxi, it was a private car with a bearded
man at the wheel. Joanna knew, without a shadow of doubt,
that it was this man, not Carlo César, to whom Marc had
telephoned from the café. She expected him to get into the
car but he did not do so; he merely thrust the travel-bag
through the open window.

Suddenly somebody was shouting, 'No, stop! What are
you doing. Stop!' Yes, it was her own voice, and she was
running towards the car: running and screaming like a
maniac. Marc turned, shocked. The car began to move.

'Give me that film! What are you doing? *Stop!*' She had
been seized and was being held, legs flailing, still trying to
propel her body forward. The car was now pulling away; a
bearded face glanced back. Marc, struggling with her, to
the amusement and amazement of passers-by, said, 'Be
quiet! This is dangerous. I can explain.'

Explain! She stopped struggling. He released her. She hit
him as hard as she could, aiming viciously for his bruised
eye but missing it. He grabbed her again. 'Jeanne, shut *up*!
If anyone's watching . . .'

In some part of her disordered mind the warning made
sense. 'Who the hell is he, why did you give him the
film?'

'He's a friend of mine.'

'Ha! Like the one in the parking-lot!'

'What do you mean?'

'At Notre-Dame-de-la-Garde. Thickset, bald, dark-
glasses. You were talking to him when we came down at the
end of filming.'

He stared at her, bemused; then said uncertainly, 'Yes, I
. . . I did talk to a man. Not a friend, I'd never seen him
before.'

'Oh God! What kind of a dummy do you think I am?'
She swung away, but he grabbed her arm and pulled her

back, hurting her, shouting at her in French; then, more calmly: 'What are you trying to say?'

'He was in the Mercedes. He was one of the men who came after me at the airport.'

Marc stared at her, mouth slightly open. After a moment he whistled softly in amazement, a habit of his. Something about the amazement pierced her; she began to have an inkling of the fact that the demented scenario which she was intent on acting out to its end did not ring quite true. They stood staring at each other in the glaring sunlight, each searching a face thought to be well-known, and finding therein all kinds of surprises.

Marc said, 'Of course. It makes sense. If they were watching you, waiting to follow you, that's where they'd be, in the car park.'

She ignored the fact that it did indeed make sense, and continued her own prearranged performance. 'Why did you give the film to that man? Why didn't you take it to Carlo?'

'Carlo will have it in two hours—what difference will two hours make? It will be at Technicolor some time this afternoon.'

'Answer my question—why?'

'Philippe, the man in the car . . . He has a small studio here. Advertising films, technical stuff—very successful, I've directed several things for him. He's developing the film.'

'He's *what*?'

'Developing the film. We need a print.'

5

They were sitting in another café, the one at the railway station. Nothing was in the least as she had expected it to be; admittedly he had lied to her, but not for the reasons her demonic suspicion had tricked her into believing. She didn't as yet understand the true reasons, but they were not evilly inspired; he hadn't told her what he intended to do because he knew that she would strongly object: and because, whether she objected or not, he was determined to do it.

She felt as if all the bones had been removed from her body; she felt disoriented, and doubted whether life would ever return to balanced normality.

Marc was saying, 'I first thought of it when I saw your room at the Pharo. You asked me what was the matter and I said, "Nothing." I'm sorry, I should have told you then.'

She remembered the moment vividly, and even more vividly her suspicions of it in the early hours of the morning.

'And then at the flat last night, when you said the phoney policeman could have been right—the men who'd followed you didn't seem quite Monsieur Laurent's style. Remember?'

'Yes.'

'They were nothing to *do* with Laurent, that's why you thought it. Nothing that's happened has anything to do with Laurent.'

'But . . . But, Marc, it has, we know it has—the man with the ugly hands even admitted it.'

'At the airport?'

'Yes.'

'Are you sure *you* didn't mention the name first? Put it into his mind?'

She realized with a sinking heart that this was exactly what had occurred. She had said, 'You can tell Monsieur Laurent to mind his own damn business,' and the man had actually paused before picking her up on it: 'Monsieur Laurent is used to getting his own way. You would be very foolish not to give me those containers.' She nodded, but still clung to the old idea. 'He and his lawyers know exactly what the loss of that footage will do to the movie.'

'It will do nothing, Jeanne. Use your head. A second unit

could come here and pick up the long shots in half a day. What's the rest? The walls of a church in close-up. Tom could match it at a hundred churches in England, or they could rig it in the studio. A little re-cutting and Hey Presto! You know that as well as I do.'

'It wouldn't be as good.'

'And an audience would notice?'

No. She had to admit that no one would notice except a few technicians employed on the production. She shook her head uncertainly and drank some of the Coca-Cola which seemed to be on the table in front of her. The well-known taste—taste of youthful soda-fountains, taste of picnics and idle days by the pool in faraway California—seemed to have no connection with the dislocated here and now. The café was noisy with impassioned Southern reunions and fare-wells. A forlorn girl hung around the neck of an embarrassed young soldier, weeping quiet tears.

Marc had leaned forward, eyes shining; he couldn't keep the excitement out of his voice: 'Jeanne, it's something to do with the film itself.'

'This friend of yours, he won't wreck the negative?'

'Of course not, he's an expert.'

'Why do you need a print anyway, what does it matter?'

'It matters a lot. Don't you see? Somebody powerful wants it badly—they've done a lot of extraordinary things, dangerous things, trying to get their hands on it.'

'No, I don't see. Let's just send it to London and have done with it.'

Marc shook his head and leaned yet closer. 'We've got to find out *why* they want it.'

Though she was still debilitated by lying awake half the night tormented by poisonous suspicions, her brain seemed at last to be moving again; she thought she could understand what he was getting at, and didn't in the least like what she understood.

He said, 'Jeanne—once we know what's so important

about the film we can hold these people to ransom, we can make a lot of money out of it.'

She stared at him in silence, appalled by the new face which had suddenly been revealed to her. 'But . . . but that's blackmail, that's immoral!'

'So what's wrecking your hotel room? What's trying to crash your car off the road? What's dressing as cops and beating us up?'

'Marc, don't try to bullshit *me*! Just because *they're* a bunch of crooks it doesn't license us to copy them.'

'It certainly licenses me.'

'Okay, you're on your own.'

'What's this? The Great American Puritan Conscience?'

'Better than the Great European lack of one.'

'Know your problem? You're spoiled, all of you. You haven't had armies marching through your villages for a couple of thousand years—occupations, looting . . .'

'Oh, for God's sake!' They had met on this particular battlefield before.

'Me,' he said, a finger to his chest, 'I'm a peasant—we're the ones who always suffer. It's taught us to get by any damn way we can, and if that includes making a fast buck, so much the better.'

She spread her hands, not only because she was too weary to find the right reply but because she could dimly apprehend, following her months in these old, worn countries, that he had a point; but if Americans *were* spoiled it was only because many of their forefathers had been clever enough to flee the very wars and persecutions he was talking about.

More gently he said, 'When you feel better you'll see I'm talking sense.'

'I won't and you're not.'

'But we hold the Ace. Maybe four Aces.'

She could tell from his radiant face that he would never understand why the whole idea was ridiculous as well as

immoral. It was as old as the difference between men and
women, and as vast. Men caught fire at a crazy idea like
this, whereas women saw the impossibility from the start;
and were usually right. She merely said, 'Marc, the film
isn't ours, it ought to be in London anyway.'

'It *will* be in London this afternoon, but we'll have a
print.'

'That isn't . . . isn't right.'

'Not right to play your hand when you hold all the Aces!'
He laughed like a young boy. Of course he did, he was
obsessed by a stupid boyish idea just as she, only a few
minutes ago, had been obsessed by a stupid suspicion. She
realized that his very ingenuousness was prodding her back
to life, arousing something like anger in the numb interior
of her being. She too leaned forward. 'Marc, I don't want
anything to do with it.'

'You will, you will.'

'I won't, I won't. And if you go ahead I'll tell you what
I'll do—catch the first plane back to Los Angeles.' Even as
she said it she knew that she would do no such thing. In the
first place she didn't want to leave him, let alone on the
brink of this childish and perilous gamble. Secondly, she
had no intention of abandoning any part of *The Sleeping Dog*
which, via its Producer, was her stepping-stone to higher
things.

She was still struggling with this old contradiction in
terms when she noticed the expression on Marc's face; he
was staring beyond her in astonishment, disbelief, shock.
She turned to see what it was that he saw: nothing except
a man at the table behind them reading a newspaper. When
she turned back Marc had gone. Where? He was at a
bookstall in the corner. He came towards her, staring at *Le
Provençal,* bumping sightlessly into tables, into people, his
face aghast. He sat down and looked at her blankly; then
showed her the headline. She couldn't understand what it
said but there beneath it were two photographs which she

recognized at once: jolly Carlo César, beaming, and the Bardot-type secretary, pouting. She heard Marc say, 'They've been killed.'

Police are investigating the murder of Monsieur Carlo César, aged 38, well-known and popular owner of a freight agency at Marseille-Marignane, and that of his secretary, Mademoiselle Marie-Louise Gramont, aged 25.

The bodies were discovered when fire broke out at the agency at 7.0 a.m. this morning, but a police spokesman has stated that Monsieur César and Mademoiselle Gramont were probably shot at close quarters very much earlier, even as early as last night.

The effect of the fire, caused, it is said, by an incendiary device with a delayed-action mechanism, makes it difficult to ascertain the exact time of death. However, it is thought that a more detailed post mortem will give the answer.

As to motive, police are still baffled, but have not ruled out theft, since such agencies occasionally handle goods of great value. In this case, the fire would have been used to eliminate fingerprints and other incriminating evidence. A second possibility is that the fire may have been started in order to destroy some cargo or package which in itself provided evidence of another crime.

Either way the ruse proved successful, since the agency and everything in it was completely destroyed. The two bodies, though badly burned, escaped destruction because they lay in a passage, leading to the office.

Police request any clients of Monsieur César who have recently entrusted him with freight to find out whether or not it has arrived at its destination. If it has not, they are advised to contact the police at . . .

There was much more, but Marc did not translate it. Joanna was remembering that on the previous day she had not wanted to go near the freight area because of its remoteness and the ease with which she could have been attacked there, unnoticed. She said, 'You were right. If we'd let . . . them, whoever they are, take the film this wouldn't have happened.' ('If,' echoed her mother's voice, 'the most useless word in the language.')

'It could have happened for some entirely different reason —nothing to do with the film.'

'You think so?'

He sighed. 'No, I don't think so.'

They looked directly at each other: grey eyes and brown eyes searching one another for answers, for reassurances, both of them aware of the paper-thin ice over which they had been skating for nearly twenty-four hours, both aware of the danger which threatened them and which had now shown its face to be that of death.

Reading her expression as he always could, he said, 'Don't start blaming yourself, that makes no sense.'

'I know it.' But it was reasonable to mourn the happy little man and his chubby girlfriend.

'If we'd already given the film to Carlo, knowing what we know, then we could *really* blame ourselves—it would be our fault, not somebody else's mistake.'

'Get it back from The Beard, Marc—we're sending it to London straight away.'

'How? Carlo had the Customs clearance, it was burnt with everything else.'

'The Production Office can get a new one.'

'French and British, it'll take three or four days.'

And that, she thought, suits you just fine, doesn't it? The film would have to stay in Marseille until clearance was obtained, and Marseille was exactly where he wanted it for the furthering of his demented plan. She said, 'Listen— you've got to drop this idea of getting money out of these people. You'll end up dead.'

'No, rich.' Seeing the look in her eye, he added quickly,

'You can bury the Puritan Conscience, Jeanne—they're not just crooks, they're murderers.'

'And guess who's next on the list?'

'They won't kill *us*—don't you see why? We're the only people who know where the film is, and very soon now—' he glanced at his watch—'we'll know why they want it so badly.'

Joanna shook her head.

'What's that supposed to mean?'

Once again, there was no point in answering. Men were truly extraordinary; could it be possible that they did in fact belong to some other, alien species? His face was alight with excitement and expectation; he was actually enjoying this insane situation, enjoying the danger. He'd deny it of course, they always did. She said, 'Marc, come down to earth, the altitude's got to you. What do you think you're going to *find* on that film?'

'I don't know until I see it. Perhaps . . . something up at Notre-Dame which shouldn't have been there—a car, a . . . a suitcase left in a corner. Or something missing which *should* have been there. I don't know.' He gesticulated and leaned close again, fixing her with the eyes which had so often seemed gentle and understanding, but which were now, to her, the eyes of a male, chauvinist maniac. 'I tell you one thing—after this, we keep that negative too. We wouldn't send it to London even if we could. Know why?'

'No.' She was prepared for any inanity.

'Because it's our Life Insurance.'

Not so inane. Less and less inane the more she considered it. He nodded to himself, pleased by her speechless reaction.

Yes, he was right. And on this simple and preposterous premise she was going to have to accept the entire preposterous situation on his preposterous terms. Had she any option? None. Immoral or not—none.

Alors, as the French were so fond of saying, she would go along with him for a rag-bag of conflicting reasons: She loved him, no doubt about that, no sense in evading it, and could perhaps stop him making a fool of himself or even getting himself killed: she had no intention of leaving Marseille until the film had been received in London: the death of Carlo César and the destruction of their Customs clearance meant that days must pass before this could be accomplished: there was also the little matter of her ambition which was inextricably entangled with the film's eventual, and safe, arrival at Technicolor: there was even (though she would never have admitted it, and possibly wasn't even aware of it as yet) more than a shred of natural human curiosity, and, she was ashamed to discover, it seemed to be stronger than conscience. What on earth *was* hidden inside those two round flat canisters which had run away with her life and were now holding her to ransom?

THREE: LONG SHOT—ROOF-GARDEN

1

'Philippe Dinon et Cie' announced the sign: no indication that it was a small film studio, it might as well have been a fruit-packing plant or a factory producing plastic flower-pots. Joanna found this reticence reassuring; 'they' probably didn't even know that the place existed, stuck out here in La Rose, a suburb which did not live up to its pretty name. It was the furthest northward extension of the city: a jumble of utilitarian apartment buildings, blank concrete blocks, dumped higgledy-piggledy among what had once been pleasant villas clustered about a small and unassuming village.

The first thing which greeted them, from Philippe Dinon's desk facing the door through which they must enter, was a copy of *Le Provençal*: black headline above the photographs of Carlo César and his secretary. However little Marc had told this thin, tall, bearded young man about the job in hand, it had been enough for him to realize that what he was being asked to do was dangerous. Their reception could not have been called cordial, and the exchange which ensued between the two Frenchmen started icily and swiftly became overheated.

Seeing Joanna's mystified expression, Philippe said, 'Mademoiselle, I'm sorry, you do not speak French.'

'Just as well by the sound of it!' This made them both smile sheepishly. Marc said, 'Philippe is nervous, I don't blame him. I tell him we'll only stay here a short time and we'll take the film with us when we go.'

'I like life, you understand, Mademoiselle, I intend to live many years.'

Joanna understood precisely. Marc merely looked impatient. It seemed that the print was still being dried, it would be ready in twenty minutes. She seized this opportunity to ask if she could make the two telephone calls to London (Collect of course) which were now beginning to haunt her always active conscience. New York would simply have to wait, or perhaps the London Production Office would like to relay the news to Jack Kroll. Somehow she had the feeling that she had lost her benefactor and had missed her footing on that all-important leap from the secretarial to the executive ladder.

The man at Technicolor was professionally matter-of-fact about the delay, such things were always happening; Melanie at the Production Office was suitably appalled by the news of Carlo César's violent death, and perfectly understood that without a Customs clearance the film could not be moved; she would set about rectifying the situation right away. As for their Producer, it was her opinion, knowing how much Mr Kroll already had on his plate, that for the time being at least, ignorance would be bliss. Joanna agreed wholeheartedly.

Melanie said, 'Jo, how do I get hold of you? Give me a number.'

'I don't have a number. You can't.'

'Well then, for God's sake call *me*.'

'Okay.'

'Promise, Jo? Call me tomorrow, we've got to keep in touch.'

'I'll call you tomorrow, I promise.'

As soon as she replaced the receiver Marc said, 'It's ready, it's in the projector.'

The sense of anticipation which accompanied her into the tiny viewing-theatre was a first inkling of how strong her curiosity really was; but for some puritan reason she felt obliged to rationalize it: of course she was . . . well, intrigued, after all she was human; that didn't mean she condoned any of Marc's illegal behaviour or any of his idiotic motives; indeed, she hoped that the next hour would bring about the collapse of his crazy theory and thus save him from coming to a sticky end.

Having sat them down, Philippe said, '*Alors*, I leave it to you. I have work to do, and in any case I do not wish to see. The less I know about this affair the better.' And from the door he added that nobody would require the little theatre until five p.m.

The lights dimmed. The screen glared white, flickered raggedly, and there was young Johnny with his clapperboard: '*Sleeping Dog*. Scene 80, Take 1.'

They were back at Notre-Dame-de-la-Garde on the last day of full shooting. The Camera was behind the leading actors, 'Danielle' and 'Steven' as they began to climb the steps leading to the church. From them it panned upwards to show the heavily ornamented façade, nineteenth-century 'Romano-Byzantine', and the tower surmounted by its enormous golden statue of the Virgin, utterly out of scale with the building but much beloved by the people of Marseille. Though it was fashionable to mock Notre-Dame as an architectural monstrosity, Joanna privately thought that there was something rather splendid about it, standing high above the city, guarding it as well as the ships which constantly came and went.

This shot was repeated twice. There were then three reverse angles on 'Steven' and 'Danielle'; then four Takes of them reaching the platform on which the basilica stands. There was no sound, but dramatically this didn't matter because the sequence depended on tension not dialogue.

Once again, as always, Joanna was astounded by the expertise of the two stars: they were so tiresome as people that one forgot how very good they were at their job. No onlooker could have guessed this, because at the time they had appeared to be doing little or nothing; but they were not acting for onlookers, they were acting for the ultra-sensitive eye of the Camera. And it was all there: the tension, the uncertainty, the mutual attraction which might yet be hostile. Lost in admiration, and a sucker for movies anyway, Joanna entirely forgot that the purpose of the entertainment was to search for any untowards or telltale background details. Marc, judging from his expression, was taking better care of this aspect than she could hope to do.

Now the man and woman were looking at the view: five Takes from five slightly different positions. Gulls were wheeling around them: very effective. She had forgotten the gulls, an unexpected and at first irritating presence. It was old Tom, the cameraman, who had pointed out how their criss-crossing flight and their wild screaming could be used to heighten the tension of the sequence. Nelson (Zoom-Zoom) Rocca, though no mean Director, did not have this kind of imagination, but he quickly appropriated the idea. A car was sent down to the market for some of the tiny fish which appeared on menus as *friture du golfe*, and the gulls were encouraged to give better performances by glittering silver handfuls flung skywards. The result would be even more striking when the sound-track added their harsh cries.

The sequence continued with 'Danielle' and 'Steven' going into the crypt where, under the pretence of lighting a candle, she evades him and disappears. He discovers the fact; is mystified; runs out of the crypt on to the terrace. He looks about him, sensing danger. He looks down and sees her car driving away. He turns, now extremely wary and disturbed, and runs down the steps away from the place.

How he then became involved in an 'accident' which nearly killed him had been filmed weeks earlier. This, therefore, was the end of location shooting, except for the single shot, his point of view to the car driving away, which had been left for Joanna and Marc and the camera-crew to pick up later.

The screen flickered back to white. Marc told the projectionist to hold it for a moment, and looked at Joanna. 'See
anything?'

'No, I can't say I did.' (Far too absorbed in technique!)
'That couple who walked past them in the Medium Shot
—I don't remember employing them as extras. And what
about the car?'

'What car?'

'The one which drove into the parking-lot behind them.
On the Reverse Angle, Takes Three and Four.'

Joanna looked blank. Marc did not comment, but picked
up the telephone and told the projectionist that he wanted
to see the same footage again.

This time, by a great effort of will, Joanna managed to
keep her eyes away from those two mesmeric performers.
She actually took a good look at the couple who passed them
on the steps, noticed the car which appeared behind their
backs, even saw, at one moment, a mysterious black box
reposing on the parapet of the terrace.

When it was over she was able to say, 'The couple were
obviously extras or they wouldn't have been in all three
Takes. And I know about the car—Rocca thought the shot
was lifeless so he asked for background movement. It was
one of the unit cars, some stunt-man drove it.'

Marc knew the purpose of the black box. Sound had
wanted a guide-track; it had sheltered a microphone from
the wind and had not appeared in the shot proper. He
sat hunched forward, deep in thought; then said, 'There's
nothing, is there? Just the two of them, and the walls of the
church, and a lot of sky and seagulls. We missed it.' And to
the projectionist, 'Run it again, please.'

Joanna, having so recently been in the grip of an obsession
herself, could very clearly recognize this extension of his.
She sighed quietly as the whole day's filming, another half
hour of it, flickered on to the screen yet again. She would
have liked to close her eyes, but knew that if she did so she

would probably fall asleep and be castigated by Marc for rank inattention. Instead she fell to analysing the tricks of those two consummate technicians.

When it was over, Marc shook his head gloomily; he did not even ask her if she'd seen anything of interest. 'Well, we'd better take a look at *our* little masterpiece, but I don't see how there could be anything in it.'

And so they sat and watched their work of the previous morning: 'Steven's' point of view from the terrace. In Take 1 the car was almost out of sight before the Camera reached the edge of the terrace. In Take 2 this was rectified. Take 3 included the terrible zoom which made them both groan. Take 4 was identical to Take 2. All that could be seen in any of them was the car passing the extras on the road, Montée de l'Oratoire, and a swiftly-moving background of dark pines, rocky slope, and a few red-tiled rooftops beyond.

Marc, indefatigable, asked for it to be run again. They had now been sitting in the stuffy little room for two hours. Joanna realized that they were going to continue to sit there until he saw something which proved his point; and if that didn't happen before five p.m., when Philippe needed the theatre to screen one of his ads, then they would wait outside, come back when it was all over, and continue to search, with or without a projectionist: until midnight; until dawn if necessary.

Again the spoiled Take 1. Again the perfect Take 2, and Take 3 with unnecessary zoom, and Take 4 just in case.

The lights came up. Marc looked at her inquiringly. 'Anything?'

'No. Or . . .'

'What?'

'I thought . . . I guess it doesn't mean a thing, but there seemed to be, I don't know, people on the roof of one of the houses.'

'I didn't see that.'

'Take Three. Just at the beginning of the zoom.'

They ran it again. Marc moved forward to the front row and sat there, tensed. Take 3 began; the Camera slid forward; the car shot into view; as it passed one of the extras, an old woman in black, the zoom began, and . . . Yes, no doubt about it: for a second, not longer, there was a glimpse of people in the far background beyond the almost black pine-trees; they seemed to be staring towards the Camera.

Marc swore out loud and jumped to his feet. 'Not on the roof, on some kind of terrace, a garden . . . What do you call it?'

'A roof-garden.'

'Yes.' He was excited now; he pushed his hair up from his forehead and stood staring at her, the eyes golden with fire, hair on end. 'They were only in that one Take, did you notice?'

Yes, she had noticed.

'We'll see it again.' But as he turned to the telephone he came to a stop; looked back at her. 'If . . . If there *is* anything there, we don't want anyone else to know. Right?'

She nodded, feeling fear and, yes, a definite twinge of excitement in her stomach.

'Philippe's got an old Moviola, we'll take a closer look on that.' He lifted the receiver and said to the projectionist, 'Thank you. Thank you very much. I think we can report to our Director that it's okay.'

They took the reel of film (there was not really enough of it for two cans; these had only been necessary because it had been shot on two separate days) and went in search of the Moviola. Philippe, with a shrug, gave them his permission to use it; the shrug implied that he would far rather have seen the back of them. This, had he known it, he was not going to do for some time yet.

Marc ran Takes 1 and 2 through the machine at speed, eye to the viewing aperture; then he began to run Take 3 more slowly. He stopped; reversed the run; went forward again at a snail's pace; then said something under his breath in French. He adjusted the focus and stepped away, indicating that Joanna should look; she did so, and immediately saw the white car in foreground against the darkness of pines; and above the pines a slope of tiled roof, and above that . . . Yes, certainly a roof-garden. Three figures were standing on it, apparently two men and a woman; one of the men seemed to have his back to the Camera but was perhaps in the act of turning; the other two were facing it directly and did indeed seem to be staring at it, though all their faces were little more than pink blobs.

Marc said, 'I've got a feeling that's it.'

'Could be meaningless.'

'But, Jeanne, there's nothing else—we've seen it all three times.' He looked about him, found the scissors which are never very far away in a cutting-room, and snipped out the few frames in which the people on the roof-garden made their brief appearance. Then he went in eager search of his long-suffering friend, Joanna trailing behind.

What he now wanted, naturally, was for Philippe to make some enlarged stills of a portion of the frames in question. He took a ruler and a pencil, and drew a neat oblong around the three figures. Philippe was evidently of the opinion that he had done as much as friendship demanded, perhaps more. 'And,' he added, in English for Joanna's benefit, 'all such things cost money, you know this.'

'I'll direct an ad for you free.'

Philippe ran thin fingers through his beard, looking both doubtful and unwilling.

Marc said, 'Okay, I'll direct two ads for you free.'

This, it seemed, was an offer which Philippe could not resist; he agreed to provide enlargements of three of the frames. Marc was pleased, and said, 'Oh, and Philippe? Will you do them yourself?'

'What do you think? I have a good team, I can't afford to lose any of my boys.'

Marc laughed excitedly. Philippe's eyes met Joanna's as

he turned out of the room; no words were necessary, he didn't even need to raise his eyebrows. Marc said, 'This is like *Blow-Up*, Antonioni, did you see it?'

'Sure, on TV. Sixties schmuck!'

Marc didn't agree. So it was a bit of a mess and didn't add up, but it had panache. They bickered amiably about the film, but only just amiably. His juvenile excitement was beginning to get on her nerves, partly, she had to admit, because it was highly contagious and she seemed to be catching it. In order to change the subject and thus douse the contagion with a little disinfectant reality, she said, 'I guess you realize our things are still at that crummy hotel.'

'Of course. Best place for them.'

'I'm not staying there another night.'

'No, no.' He hugged her but without thought. 'We'll find somewhere better—none of the hotels are full this time of year.' Obviously it didn't matter to him where they slept; only one thing mattered to him.

The enlargements, when Philippe finally produced them, were an eye-opener; he put them on the cutting-room table with his 'See, Hear, and Speak No Evil' expression; then left them to their own devices. Joanna wished that she could share his lack of curiosity but was now getting used to the fact that this was impossible: she was hooked. And after all, she was the one who'd actually made the discovery.

Staring at the photographs, Marc gave his little low whistle of astonishment. There must have been something about that particular zoom-lens, or about zoom-lenses in general for all Joanna knew, which lent itself to enlargement, because the pictures were unusually clear; a little fuzzy of course, due to distance, but with barely any of the grainy texture which she had expected.

The roof-garden was revealed as being altogether larger and more luxurious than it had appeared to be on film; the further end, half obscured by an awning and its deep shadow, was bordered by an arched pergola with something, perhaps roses, trained over it; there were two magnificent urns, newly planted with colour; there were many glossy and well-tended evergreens, and even a small flowering tree, plum or cherry; handsome white furniture was grouped in front of an open french window.

The man with his back to Camera was slim, young, and had indeed been caught in the act of turning: a handsome profile, black hair, muscular shoulders well-displayed by his T-shirt. The woman, they could now see, was beautiful, really remarkably beautiful, slender, dark hair fashionably cut; she wore a white dress of great simplicity and, Joanna guessed, great price; it looked as if she had just stood up from a comfortable day-bed immediately behind her. One hand was held against her throat in the classic gesture of sudden concern, and she was undoubtedly, as from the first she had seemed to be, staring directly at the Camera. So was the man beside her. And the man beside her was the grey-haired individual with the ugly hands who had confronted Joanna at the airport, demanding that she immediately give him the film.

2

The beautiful woman, whom Joanna and Marc would have recognized at once, was at that moment sitting on a balcony overlooking the courtyard of a house in the old city of Tunis. She was wearing a faultless suit the colour of dried straw which, again, Joanna would have recognized as being extremely expensive. If they had asked her name she would have told them it was Christina Neff, and her Swiss passport would have corroborated the fact. She was drinking fresh lemon-juice and Perrier, and she was thinking about freedom and age, related and important subjects as far as she was concerned: though not as important as money, and sex.

She was within a month of her thirty-eighth birthday. Many things had seemed simple and desirable at twenty-

eight: simple *because* they were desirable: but became neither
as one approached forty, the age when, it was occasionally
said, Life began. Another of those crass bits of wishful
thinking which, after they'd been repeated often enough by
enough stupid people, passed for folk wisdom.

She didn't like this house. She had only visited it once
before, and had thought then, as she thought now, that it
was typical of the man who owned it: nothing to be seen
from the outside but flaking walls and little barred windows,
and within, this extraordinary garden with its two Roman
fountains, looted from God knows where, its roses and
oleanders, palms and tamarisks and cool green ferns nodding over rivulets of water which ran here, there and every-
where. Not being an Arab she wasn't addicted to the sound
of water; didn't like the silence that lay behind it, nor the
pervading sense of secrecy.

The balcony was wide, and encircled all four sides of the
courtyard, a perfect symmetry of arches supporting yet
another arched balcony above; but if one tried to walk
around it to get a better view of the garden one came
upon iron barriers, cruelly spiked; beyond them, occupying
two-thirds of the space, was more secrecy. Women's quarters? Rooms stuffed to the ceiling with gold bars? With
corpses? She didn't know, had not been told, and wouldn't
have received a straight answer if she'd asked.

Sitting down like this she felt trapped by the place; she
stood up and began to pace to and fro, her heels clicking on
the tiled floor, probably an irritating noise to other people
within earshot who would be used to soft-soled Arab shoes
or to bare feet; she hoped so.

Freedom had changed its face, that was the point. The
carefree companion who had accompanied her, laughing
through her two marriages had become selfish and demanding now that she was on her own, and the need to escape
had become a habit; it had even driven her to this house.

Tapping backwards and forwards, she would have liked

to look closely at her face, searching it for signs of age which were barely there (one of the few practical uses of money) but of course there were no mirrors on the balcony, and she wasn't going to give anyone who was watching the satisfaction of seeing her take out a compact and examine herself in it. She knew enough about Arab houses to be sure that she was watched: hence their passion for grilles of every shape and kind.

Click-click went her heels, pleasing her. Why the hell had she become involved with Arabs anyway? Stupid question.

The man, owner of this house and others, who came through an archway behind her was undoubtedly of Arab extraction, well mixed, but as far as his acquaintances in the casinos and marinas of the world were concerned he might as well have been South American or Greek—who cared, he was rich? His name was Paul Nogaro, but he was known as Benny. The 'Nogaro' made people think; he had chosen it for that purpose. Japanese, Italian? On the contrary, it was a small town in the Gers region of France which he had known, briefly, during a period of enforced rustication following some misjudged escapade of his youth.

He was now sixty-four years old, a big man but not fat; he had grey curly hair cut short; he looked, particularly in the djelabah which he always wore in Tunis, like a Roman Emperor—a hard-headed, sane, but possibly cruel one.

'Madame.'

'Benny. Thank you for sending the plane, that was generous.' They both knew that there wasn't a trace of generosity in his character; if he had sent his private plane to collect her from Nice he had done so for his own personal reasons. He gestured to the chairs; they sat down. He snapped his fingers, and a willowy boy appeared, downcast eyes fringed by enormous lashes. The woman wanted another Perrier and lemon-juice, it was hot in Tunis. Her host commanded a gin-fizz; then said, 'Thank you for coming to see me.' They both knew that her reasons for coming were also purely selfish; she was dissatisfied, 'pissed off' was the expression she had used on the telephone, with his son's behaviour. Since he too was dissatisfied with Leo's behaviour, from a different and more profound point of view, he was interested in what she had to say.

He waited until the boy had materialized with their drinks, until he had disappeared, before continuing: 'Perhaps we will speak English; nobody here speaks English.'

She shrugged. English, French, Italian, Greek, it made little difference to her; she could also have managed in Spanish and German, but less expertly.

His English was ramshackle, with American overtones, learned God knew where: 'The whole darn thing sounds careless, stoopid. Not like you.'

'Benny, I was so *tired* of being cooped up in that apartment. And the Mistral, oh God!'

He nodded, knowing all about the Mistral; but what would a north wind matter to this woman from the North, she ought to be used to such things? And anyway, she and his son had only just returned from the Caribbean, latest of many jaunts which in part explained why Leo was not on top of his work. If she had ever, for two weeks on end, stayed in the Marseille apartment he could understand her feeling constrained, but even when Leo pulled himself together and took up residence for a while she was always elsewhere, kept in expensive seclusion, naturally.

She was saying, 'We were told they'd gone two days ago. *Le Provençal* said they'd gone, so did television.'

'And?'

'Well, the sun came out, so hot, so beautiful, you know how it is in April, and I just *had* to go and lie in it.'

He regarded her, eyes half-closed, and nodded. This kind of Northern woman was unbalanced when it came to the sun, which all Southerners knew to be an enemy; or if a friend, one to be treated with caution. They came rushing down from their grey, damp marshes, spreading themselves out to dry like so much wet linen, and were not content until they had grilled themselves to the unattractive colour of stained oak. Well, to be fair, this one never went that far, being too aware of her beauty and of what the sun could do to it. But certainly she would run out on to the terrace at the first sign of spring sunshine.

As for her dislike of being 'cooped up' in his son's apartment, that was entirely her own fault; if they had either of them spent a little more time thinking and a little less time thrashing about in bed they could have foreseen a great many avoidable mistakes; they might even have foreseen that the whole idea was doomed to failure.

Ah no, he was forgetting. They were both on khif at the time, stoned. His son, in the name of God! Any sane person who dealt in heroin surely knew better than to play around with drugs? Not Leo. And surely any rich young man knew that when you passionately desired a woman like this you took her by force, or paid her, and threw her out next morning? Not Leo. As quietly as if none of these things tormented him, he said, 'And they hadn't gone.'

'No. Of course I didn't know the camera was there or I'd never have gone out—it was hidden. Then I looked up and saw the sun catching something bright. I called Leo, he was talking to Zizi in the apartment. He fetched his binoculars, and then we knew for certain. He said the camera was pointing straight at us.'

'From a great distance.'

'Yes, but there was some special lens—a telescopic lens, he said—he could see it quite clearly.'

'Why? And why could anyone see *you*? There's a screen.'

'It hadn't been put up. Last year apparently the Mistral wrecked it.'

'So you were overlooked by the whole of Notre-Dame.'

'Not the whole of it, just that particular part. Yes, I know I was silly.'

'Silly's kind of a mild word for it.' He sipped his fizz and considered the matter with a sour expression. 'Seems to me you all acted off the top of your heads, like a bunch of dumb kids.'

'Benny, I did so hope you'd say that.' When she smiled he had to admit to himself, if unwillingly, that she was a very attractive woman. 'I told them and told them, "Leave it alone, it doesn't matter," but you know what Leo's like —and Zizi's a fool, I don't know why you employ him.'

'Leo employs him.'

She smiled again, confidentially, implying that everybody knew Leo was just his son, a lucky and spoiled young man unable to hold the reins of a power which was constantly plunging off-course and dragging him with it. He resented her criticism but feared she was correct. 'They didn't listen?' He wouldn't have listened himself, but then he would never have allowed such a situation to arise.

'No. They picked up a couple more men and went tearing up to Notre-Dame in the Mercedes, and then chased this wretched girl to the airport. Of course she wondered what the hell was going on—lost her head—called in her boy-friend. If they'd let her send the damned film to England nobody would have given it a second thought. And we're not even sure it *shows* anything!'

She was right, of course. He knew a little about filming, having once misguidedly invested money in a production. Not that it mattered; the Producer, another acquaintance, an American, remained in his debt; one day he would ask for the debt to be honoured, not in money of course, he had long since written off the money, but in some other way still unknown. He was an inveterate collector of such obligations; it was extraordinary how useful they proved to be. 'And now Leo says these youngsters have disappeared.'

'By God, wouldn't *you*? Or didn't he tell you about that mayhem at the airport.'

A heavy nod was all the reply she got to this. Leo had not in fact mentioned the senseless murder of Carlo César

and his secretary, aware of how much it would unfuriate his
father; but there had been other calls from Marseille apart
from those made by his son and by this woman; there was
little, ever, that he didn't hear almost immediately. 'Nobody
seems to know whether the boy and girl even *have* the film.'

'Nobody's sure of anything, Benny.'

He sighed deeply.

'Left alone, neither of them would have done a thing. As
it is . . .' The elegant hand described a fluttering gesture of
turmoil.

'You're kind of being wise after the event.'

'I'm being wise after the non-event which Leo and Zizi
turned into an event. Now it's in the lap of the gods—
whether they find what's on the film, *if* it's on the film—
whether they know what it means.'

'Whether *you're* on the film and what *you* mean.'

She met the hooded eyes directly. Of course this was what
concerned her and of course he knew it. 'Your son,' she said
coolly, 'isn't exactly uninvolved.'

He permitted himself a small mirthless smile. 'Poor kid!
He was led astray by this older woman, thirteen years older,
an . . . adventuress. He thought it was all a big joke, he had
no idea it was for real.'

She matched his smile, and added, 'But he came out of
it half a million dollars richer—poor kid!'

He loved his son, though it was only at moments like this
that he realized how much: an only son, product of that late
marriage to a beautiful girl with no brain: now fat and
discontented, immured in the women's quarters on the other
side of the courtyard. The only son had been pampered and
spoiled: expensive schools, too much money, not enough
discipline. He himself had behaved like any stupid and rich
bourgeois father, he the slum-boy who had slaved and
sometimes starved for every penny he'd made. The sons of
such men invariably behaved like princes, proving nothing
except that their fathers were old fools.

The truth was that when his lifelong friend, Rico Milliard, had tripped over the Law and fallen into the pigsty for ten years he should never have entrusted Marseille to Leo. Fatherly love and fatherly pride had blinded him, and now, perhaps very soon, he was going to have to pay for that blindness.

He finished his drink and peered at his son's mistress through the empty glass. She was exactly the kind of woman Leo needed; though Leo was naturally unaware of the fact, and she was tired of Leo. 'So,' he said, 'what you want is for *me* to make sure this piece of film, which may or may not have your face on it, isn't used against you.'

'Against Leo and me. His face would be there too.'

'You don't think he can take care of it himself?'

'He's proved he can't, he and that ox Zizi between them.'

'The American girl and her boyfriend are kids, nothings, how could they be dangerous?' He knew the answers and only wanted to find out if she did.

'Benny.' Knowing that he knew she could afford to treat him like a kid himself. 'There was rough-stuff, they tried to grab the film, they ransacked her room at the Pharo, they played silly games pretending to be the police. So the boy and girl start wondering. They take a look at the film, searching for things. If Leo and I are on it they may add two and two . . .'

'If. May.'

'You want to take chances?'

He didn't reply.

'If they see us they wonder who the hell we are, why the hell Zizi made such a fuss. They also recognize the roof-garden—they look for it—they find it—it's part of an apartment belonging to Leo Nogaro. Christ! Already they know too much, even if they *don't* recognize me.'

Another of those heavy nods; another sharp glance from half-closed eyes.

'Because they're the only people who will connect the film

with those deaths at the airport, they're the only people who
can. And if they've *got* the film they hold proof.'

'Maybe. And maybe you and Leo are imagining too
much.'

'I'm sure as hell not imagining that two innocent people
were murdered at Marignane.'

He sat for a time in silence, an ageing man who no longer
had any patience with this kind of stupidity. Killing always
bred killing, but Leo had never understood that. He himself
didn't in the least want to pass the death sentence on the
young American girl and her French lover, yet he could see
a situation arising in which he would have no option but to
do so: and all for a beloved son with no brain and a woman
whom he disliked. He said, 'I guess we have to make a
deal.'

'Certainly.'

'I take care of this goddam cock-up, you never go near
my son again.'

Her eyes told him that the arrangement suited her perfectly and was all to her advantage; so did the speed with
which she said, 'Done! Let's drink to that.'

He let her drink alone since his glass was empty.

She had been thinking for a long time now about the
United States, a vast and busy country in which one could
lose oneself so easily. Neither of her husbands had spent
much time there, quick trips to New York and Washington,
with the result that she knew very few Americans who
actually lived there, though many who didn't, and they were
all confined to the East Coast. Moreover, Mexico and Brazil
were only a step away. She was sick to death of having dark
hair and wanted to go back to her natural blonde, which
made her look younger anyway; also, the damned contact
lenses, though she had now grown used to them, were a
constant bore.

Perhaps she was even old enough and experienced enough
to have learned from her mistakes; she would never again

become involved with a man, only with men, as many different ones as possible, this being the kind of freedom she required; and as for age, well, everybody had to come to terms with that old bitch one way or another, and she wasn't doing too badly as yet . . .

He interrupted her thoughts by saying, 'You get the best of the bargain, but as we know, I'm a generous man.'

'Dear Benny—*so* generous.'

'I'm thinking of Mr Foxley.'

Her smile did not even waver, for which he really admired her; in fact she even managed to laugh lightly before replying, 'But of course—we both are. I wonder if his ears are burning.'

3

Before leaving Philippe Dinon's tiny film studio Marc returned to the cutting-room where he took certain precautions. He removed the third Take, the one with the telltale zoom, from both the negative and the print, and he also removed the words which followed it, 'Scene 93, Take 4'. The result of this operation was that Take 4 now followed the words, 'Scene 93, Take 3' and therefore appeared to *be* that Take.

Watching this, Joanna wondered what sort of condition the negative would be in by the time it reached Technicolor; the team of perfectionists employed there would not be pleased to find that it had been processed elsewhere, possibly without their customary finesse, and Nelson Rocco would certainly want to know what had happened to his precious zoom. All Miss Production Co-ordinator would be able to do was to rely on the confusion caused by Carlo César's death, and on any likely stories which came to mind when this entire muddle hit the fan. In any case, London and the Studio and the resumption of shooting on *The Sleeping Dog* all seemed unimaginably far away. A lot of things could happen before then; she and Marc could even be dead before then.

He had now put the excised negative and print into a small canister on their own; he then sealed the rest of the negative into a second, much larger can, and the rest of the print into a third. He put all this, with the enlarged stills, into the travel-bag, and, to Philippe's very evident relief, they removed both themselves and the evidence from his premises.

Sitting side by side on the Métro on their way back to Marseille they spoke very little; and what they said was a strange kind of echo of words already spoken five hundred miles away on the African shore of the Mediterranean. From Joanna, 'I don't get it. Why didn't they just let me send it off to London? I mean, who'd have noticed or cared? And the zoom-shot won't be used anyway, it's too corny.'

'I suppose it's a risk they can't afford to take.'

'Who do you think they are, Marc, the woman and the young man in that picture?'

'That's what we're going to find out—that's the next step.'

She sighed, realizing that whereas she had said 'you' he had said 'we'. He knew as well as she did that she was hooked. She would like to have added, once again, 'You were right first time—let's just allow them to grab it,' but once again she didn't do so for the old well-worn reason which now appeared more than ever morally reprehensible. Perhaps she had lived so long with her ambition that she'd be unwilling to relinquish it even at gun-point: something she might yet be requested to do.

Searching for self-excuse, she turned to Marc's European rationale: they were dealing with crooks and killers, and therefore their own crooked behaviour was permissible. It was a persuasive idea, but alas, her ever-nagging conscience suggested that she only found it so because it was convenient. On the practical level, however, there were no doubts;

somehow, at some future moment, she must at all costs deflect his half-witted idea of making money out of Scene 93, Take 3. Moral issues apart, their adversaries would certainly outwit him and probably kill him.

He, needless to say, was thinking along opposite lines. There's one big problem, when it comes to identifying that couple on the roof—we can't use any of the obvious sources, newspapermen, police. We'd have to show them our pictures, and that would be the end of that.

Was there perhaps a hope that he'd end up stifling his lurid plan in its own secrecy? Apparently not. 'I've been thinking about . . . the sister of my grandmother. You'd call her my Great-aunt Claudine, yes? She is seventy-two. She reads all the scandal, everything—it's her hobby. There's a chance she'll recognize one of them.' He was smiling. 'You'll like her, Jeanne, she's very rich and amusing. The great character of my mother's family.'

Joanna had assumed that Madame Argenti of the Bar des Moulins was probably the great character of his mother's family, but in her present state she would have liked nothing better than to visit a very rich great-aunt, amusing or not, and to use her rich bathroom, and even to sleep and sleep in one of her rich, soft beds.

Marc said, 'Later, not now,' thus deflating the opulent balloon. 'Now there is work to do.'

They had arrived at St Charles. They left the Métro and ascended to the railway station which, Joanna thought, seemed to be a kind of recurring motif in their tortuous life. Once again the travel-bag was entrusted to the bureaucratic Dobermans within their compound. As they turned away, Marc slipping the new receipt into his wallet, she said, 'Where now?' She was thinking of a large cup of coffee and perhaps a Danish pastry.

Marc replied, 'Notre-Dame-de-la-Garde—before the light goes.'

4

In London, Charles Foxley was wondering whether he would dine at his Club or cook himself a couple of poached eggs in the blessedly deserted kitchen. The answer depended on when the telephone calls came through and on how long they took.

On Thursdays Kevin, his manservant, had the evening off. Not that he didn't trust Kevin, up to a point, and not that the calls didn't come in on his own private line, no extensions. One could not be too careful; Charles Foxley had learned that from life, by God, if he had learned nothing else.

He thought with pleasure of the empty kitchen, silent except for the ticking of the clock. On a Thursday the Club would be almost as empty and as silent, a majority of members having already scurried away to various country retreats. On Fridays they were absent from their offices, one of the reasons that Britain was down the drain, one of the reasons that Charles Foxley was richer than they were; he always worked until five p.m. five days a week.

He too possessed a country retreat, twelve bedrooms, as well as another in Bermuda, though these days he seldom visited either. He liked being alone, always had, just as he'd always disliked servants and, particularly, the service for which one paid them: yet another of those contradictions in terms bestowed so liberally by life: by his life anyway.

Whether he stayed in Eaton Square or went to the Club he would first of all take a bath and put on a dressing-gown. He removed his dark City suit, dark tie, white shirt, black shoes, and stood regarding his reflection with candid distaste. In vest and underpants and black socks few men present an impressive figure; he thought, not for the first time, that he looked more like an accommodating suburban Bank Manager (if there was any such thing these days) than what the newspapers called a 'multi-millionaire'. Occasionally they made guesses as to the exact extent of his wealth but these were always far wide of the mark, mostly, thank heaven, underestimating his true worth.

No, not impressive, he thought, eyeing the slight stomach and tucking it in, eyeing the sturdy legs which were a little too short for the long body, just as the head was a little too large for the whole ensemble. However, the head was at least in its own way striking: square-jawed, with sandy-grey hair brushed back from a high forehead, greenish eyes the colour of snow-water, a straight, commanding nose, a straight mouth which could, when it smiled, be charming. Perhaps it was the mouth that some women found attractive. He grimaced at his reflection, mocking it. No, it was his money that some women found attractive.

He was still examining himself without satisfaction when the first call came through. 'Hollis, sir. Good evening.'

'Where are you now?'

'Vienna. Nothing to report, sir, I'm afraid.'

'I forget about your contacts in Vienna.'

'Very good, sir. Excellent. If there was anything to be known they'd know it.'

Still in underwear and socks, he had gone to his desk in the study. He opened an atlas and stared at it, frowning. Hollis was saying, 'I followed up the Munich lead—there was nothing to that either.'

'I think,' said Charles Foxley, eyes on the atlas, 'that I'd like you to go to Gstaad.'

'Yes, sir.'

'And round about.'

'Yes, sir.'

'Expenses?'

'One thousand, seven hundred, sir. I had to go back to Hamburg if you remember.'

Foxley opened a notebook and wrote, *Week ending 20 April. Hollis £1,700. To Gstaad.* He said, 'Very good, Hollis. Until next Thursday.'

'Yes, sir. Good night, sir.'

Three bags full, sir. He wished that Hollis didn't sound so like a policeman, but that could hardly be held against him since he was, in fact. ex-CID, dispensed with for irregularities which even the Metropolitan force could hardly overlook. However, he was thorough, never cheated on his expenses, didn't always stay at the best hotels and eat at the best restaurants: unlike Duncliffe who would, as usual, be the last to report, even though he was only in Madrid.

'Nothing to report, I'm afraid.' It was invariably the same, but then it was invariably the same for all businessmen with worldwide interests who maintained their own worldwide intelligence networks.

Next came Mackenzie from Rabat; nothing to report; he would now move eastwards through Tangier. Clark, from Mombasa, had nothing to report either; he could go back to Cape Town. As for Edmonds, from Washington DC, he could damn well come home and seek other employment: the US was expensive but not that expensive! Malin had nothing to report from Bangkok, but wanted to follow up an interesting lead in Singapore. Perry, almost incoherent from Melbourne, could have been drunk or speaking, as he claimed, via a disintegrating satellite; there seemed little point in keeping him in Australia, but he might as well go back to Sydney for another week at least. Passmore, from Martinique, had nothing to report.

Finally, long after Charles Foxley had bathed and put on his dressing-gown, Duncliffe rang from Madrid, very terse and businesslike. Foxley was never sure about Duncliffe, though his Secret Service credentials had turned out to be genuine; no reason was given for the termination of his employment, but then they never gave reasons. Research had proved that he had indeed, as claimed, gone to Eton and Trinity. With all these justifications there was still something about him which didn't ring true, but what did that matter? He was efficient, he knew a great many influential people.

Needless to say, he had nothing to report. 'Thought I might sort of drift down towards Lisbon, Estoril.'

'No. I want you to go to France—along the coast.'

'Again?'

'Again.'

'You're the boss.'

'Expenses?'

'Five thousand one hundred. My contact here's a bit grand—doesn't do it for peanuts. Then there was Seville and Granada. Damn cold in Granada!'

Requiring, Charles Foxley thought, plenty of brandy— cognac, not that Spanish muck—as well as something nubile on which to warm one's feet in bed. Was Duncliffe worth it? Hard to tell. Hard to tell if any of them were worth it until one of them came up trumps. Intelligence, like everything else, was a gamble.

'Ring you next Thursday, then.'

'Please.'

He closed the atlas and put the notebook on top of it, tidily. Then he cooked himself two poached eggs and ate them with three pieces of toast, sitting at the kitchen table. Then he brushed his teeth and went to bed. He read Dickens for half an hour—*Great Expectations*, his favourite—took the sleeping-tablet without which, these days, he tossed and turned half the night, and switched off the bedside lamp.

Sometimes he lay awake until he heard Kevin return, but tonight he fell asleep quickly. He dreamed of a telephone kiosk on the edge of a canal in Amsterdam. He was watching it from a distance. Suddenly it exploded in a huge ball of fire. But there had been somebody inside it, and now they were capering about, shouting and laughing, ignoring the fact that flames were consuming their clothes and their flesh. He realized that this person was himself.

5

By the time Joanna and Marc had toiled up the steps to Notre-Dame-de-la-Garde the sun was low over the gulf; it was a brilliantly clear evening but the shadows in the city were strong and dark: and misleading.

At first, even with the aid of the enlarged stills, they could not place the roof-garden at all. Joanna said, 'This is silly. The Camera began to zoom when the car was passing that extra, the old lady in black. She was just about there, where the steps come to an end.'

They looked upwards from the foot of the steps, past the clustering pines, almost black by this light, to the houses which could be seen above them. There were various terraces and small gardens, and tree-tops bright with fresh new leaf or late blossom, but of the roof-garden no sign at all.

So then they did something they had vowed not to do, considering it foolhardy and likely to attract attention: they put two francs into the nearest of the viewing telescopes which had been fixed at various points around Notre-Dame for the benefit of tourists. Even then, taking it in turns to search as the shadows deepened, they could not find what they were looking for. The awning would be rolled up at this time of day, and the white furniture perhaps taken indoors, but the arched pergola should have been easily distinguishable, also the pair of urns planted with bright colour, also the small blossoming tree.

The enlargement included a corner and part of a chimney, but this was little help; there were a dozen such chimneys, a hundred such corners.

It was Joanna who solved the mystery. 'Oh, I *see*. Look, Marc, they've put up a . . . kind of a screen.'

He looked and saw that this was exactly what had happened: a screen against wind and/or prying eyes, with a row of slender cypresses set against it. Over the top of it could be seen, but not at this hour at all clearly, the top of the arched pergola. He said, 'It's on the Boulevard André Aune.'

'If you say so—just a lot of rooftops to me.'

'No, not exactly on the Boulevard. See that line of shadow going downhill?'

She saw it.

'That's the Boulevard, and this is east of it. One of those little streets leading off to the right. Come on.'

They ran down the steps from the church, and then down the steps of the Montée de l'Oratoire past the Stations of the Cross. Under the dark grove of pines there were yet more steps, and these led to the top of the Boulevard André Aune. On the last flight, at a point where it divided into two, Joanna caught his arm and drew him to a standstill.

'What's the matter?'

She wasn't quite sure; couldn't exactly define the uneasiness which had gripped her. 'This is . . . dangerous.'

'To walk down a street?'

'For *us* to walk down this street. So close to that place.'

'But we've got to find out where it is, who lives there. We've got to.'

'I guess so, but . . . if we're seen poking about . . . We'd be giving ourselves away completely.'

'Why should anyone see us—it would be the most incredible coincidence.'

'They could be . . . waiting for us.' The thought made her shudder.

'Why? They don't know we printed the negative, they certainly can't know we found anything on it.'

She allowed the force of his impatience to drag her forward, but although she had expressed herself badly, didn't even know what it was that worried her, it seemed that she hadn't been completely ignored; for at the bottom of the steps, with the Boulevard sloping away from them towards the town, he came to a stop himself and stared at her, thinking. Eventually, and unwillingly: 'Yes, I see what you mean:' He turned and looked longingly down the street. Because of the gradient and because they were standing at the very top of it, they were only a little lower than the terrace on which the roof-garden had been constructed. It was at the back of a large and prosperous-looking block of apartments, facing south-east; therefore they could only see the side of it, the newly erected screen, painted the same colour as the wall and seeming to be an extension of it, and the row of cypresses placed there for decoration. As he had suspected, the building was not on the Boulevard itself, but on a small side-street.

He turned back and looked at her. '*I* could go, you could keep out of the way.'

'No, Marc.'

'It will soon be dark.'

'Marc, no. They could recognize you as easily as they could me.'

He nodded, but repeated doggedly, 'We've got to find out who lives there.'

In the end they reached a compromise. In gathering darkness they walked quickly past the road on which the building stood; it was called Rue du Palais, presumably because the Palais de Justice was situated just below and beyond, and it joined another road which went looping away in the opposite direction towards the foot of the bastion surmounted by Notre-Dame.

The Boulevard André Aune seemed to have escaped the later destructions of the city, and contained some dignified houses and a few less dignified shops. At the bottom it ran into a small square, and in the square were two cafés. They chose the nearest of these, unfortunately as things were to turn out, went in and ordered a couple of beers.

Leaning on the bar, Marc said to the patron, 'Lot of fine houses around here.'

The patron replied that it had always been a nice quiet residential area.

Marc said, 'Gardens too. There's a beautiful roof-garden

in the Rue du Palais—belongs to someone pretty rich by the look of it.'

The patron eyed him in silence.

'Number Eight or Ten Rue du Palais, it must have been. Any idea who lives there?'

The patron turned away and began to wash glasses; but an old woman, standing next to them at the bar, snorted in derision over her pastis: 'Nice quiet residential area my foot! It *used* to be.' And to Marc: 'Nogaro lives there, that's who —Leo Nogaro.'

Marc choked on his beer and had to be struck sharply between the shoulder-blades. The old lady cackled, pleased to have produced so dramatic a reaction. Joanna, taking her cue from the patron, did not ask any questions until they were once more out in the street. 'Who's Nogaro?'

She listened to his reply with widening eyes; the colour seeped out of her cheeks. At the end of the recital she said, 'Okay, that's it, no more games! We'll go visit your uncle's vineyard, anything you like. The police can take that film to the airport when clearance comes through, I'm not touching it.'

'You're just tired.'

'Okay, I'm tired, but I'm not a darn fool. If you think you can take on Mr Big himself you're crazier than I thought.'

'Leo Nogaro! He's a conceited pimp with nothing between the eyes. His *father* was Mr Big, not Little Leo.'

'Marc, I won't go along with this.'

'And I thought Americans had guts.'

'Sure I've got guts, and I don't need anyone wrapping them around my neck. Come on, let's grab our bags from that *pissoir* and get the hell out of this town.'

Marc considered her in silence. He said, 'Okay, that's what we'll do.' But his eyes were bright, and the alacrity with which he'd agreed did not deceive Joanna; she knew that he had no intention of abandoning a single move in his hare-brained plan; if anything, the news that they were taking up cudgels against what sounded like the whole underworld of Marseille had only strengthened his resolve. Oh, but men were utterly insane, every single one of them!

However, since he was to all appearances conforming with her wishes, she was unable at this moment to pursue the subject any further: particularly as he now added words which she had been longing to hear for many, many hours: 'I'm starving, are you?'

'To death.'

'Why don't we eat now? We can collect our things from the *pissoir* any time.'

So they walked down to the Place Thiars, an attractive old square, once the picturesque but seedy haunt of a hundred whores but now refurbished and repaved and liberally dotted with restaurants. Ignoring the fact that they were fast running out of cash and would need to go to a Bank first thing in the morning, they browsed among the menus, picked the one which took their fancy, and treated themselves to a well-deserved feast: the first proper meal which either of them had eaten in two days.

Then, feeling pleasantly drowsy, both of them looking forward to baths and bed in a very much better and sweeter-smelling establishment than the Métropole-St Charles, they took a taxi and went to collect the baggage which they had left there. The taxi-driver was dour and possibly knew things about the hotel which they did not; hearing the destination, he gave them a suspicious glance, presumably decided that what they got up to there was none of his business, and indicated that they might get into his vehicle. He didn't look like it, and there was no earthly reason why they should suspect it, but he was about to turn into a kind of Fairy Godmother.

6

'Zizi' Lacombe, of the ugly hands and the matt black eyes which had so alarmed Joanna at the airport, had been christened Jean-Marie. Even if he had not, in his youth, been remarkable for very long legs, the Jean-Marie alone might have caused his friends to associate him with the dancer, Zizi Jeanmaire; as it was, the legs clinched the deal, and he had been known as Zizi ever since, the joke being sharpened by the fact that he was everything she was not: graceless and plain and decidedly unsexy.

He was sitting in a big Citroën parked nearly opposite the Hôtel Métropole-St Charles, considering his day. The job hadn't proved all that difficult once he'd traced the number of Marc Gérard's car. He had at his disposal a network of informants, and one of them had soon discovered the Fiat parked in a side-street. Admittedly there were a hundred or so hotels in the vicinity of the railway station, but some of these could be discarded because they only welcomed prostitutes and their clients, and yet others because the girl and the young man, having abandoned his flat, would have found them too squalid.

It had been easy work to question the owners or managers of those that remained; all these gentlemen could well remember a certain Hôtel Perdrix which, only last year, had caught fire one night because its proprietor had displeased Leo Nogaro; six people had been burned to death and the building reduced to a pile of charred rubble surmounted by a chamber-pot, miraculously unbroken. So that when Zizi or his lieutenant, Julien (whom Joanna and Marc would have recognized as the 'plain-clothes policeman') appeared at various reception desks, various receptionists were quick and accurate with their answers: including the receptionist at the Hôtel Métropole-St Charles. He had immediately recognized the couple's description and had informed Zizi that though they had already paid the bill they were returning later in the day to collect their baggage.

Zizi didn't really expect to find the film in either untidily packed suitcase or in Joanna's document-case, that was too much to hope, but they were diligently searched, for the second time as far as Joanna's were concerned, in the hope of finding some indication of its whereabouts. There was always a chance that it had already been dispatched to London; if so, there would certainly be some kind of receipt among her papers. For a few seconds he thought he had actually found this; it was indeed a receipt, and under the heading of Carlo César's office at the airport, but it was dated 15 April, three days before the event. No other evidence came to light.

The cases were repacked and replaced behind the reception desk to await collection. That had been a little after midday. He had not expected the young man and the girl to reappear before evening, after dark if they had any sense. Now, at nine-thirty, he was still waiting, uneasily because he knew that his men would be getting bored and thus careless; he would have liked to visit the three who were not under his personal supervision in the car, but dared not do so for fear of being seen; the girl would recognize him at once; he wasn't a man whom people easily forgot.

At nine forty-five the taxi bearing a well-fed and well-wined, and therefore tactically unprepared, Marc and Joanna turned into the street. As directed, it stopped a little short of the hotel; Marc had already asked the surly driver to wait, since they wished to continue their journey. He and Joanna then got out and walked straight into Zizi's trap.

Neither of them noticed the nervousness of the receptionist. Marc was just about to pick up the two suitcases when a man materialized behind the desk. Both he and Joanna instantly recognized the pronounced widow's peak, seeming to cleave the sallow features.

Considering the state in which his excellent dinner had left him, Marc reacted with astonishing speed. He flung his own suitcase at the man, who ducked expertly but was still knocked a little off-balance. A gun had appeared in his hand and if he had fired it that would naturally have been the end of that; but Zizi had repeatedly emphasized that there would be no shooting, and so he didn't fire. By the time he had disposed of the suitcase, Marc had turned towards the double plate-glass doors and, using the second suit-case as a battering-ram, was charging directly at the man who had come in behind them in order to cut off their retreat.

Joanna, up to this point, had been gazing witlessly from one adversary to the other, saying 'Oh my God!' over and over again; but now, seeing Marc's purpose, she also threw herself towards the doors. The man was already reeling backwards under Marc's weight and was in exactly the right position to receive the full impact of the second door as she thrust it open; it hit him full in the face and sent him staggering down the steps to end up with a thump flat on his back, winded and therefore temporarily *hors de combat*.

What followed was confused and dominated by a great deal of crashing and shouting. As Joanna and Marc leapt down the steps, jumped over the writhing body of the winded man, and began to run up the street, their taxi-driver, sceptical by nature, saw what could only be an absconding fare; he thrust his car into gear and accelerated forward in pursuit. At the same moment the Citroën, with Zizi inside it, pulled out from the other side of the narrow street, also in pursuit. The taxi banged into it and slewed it sideways, wedging it firmly between two parked cars. Nor was this all, as Zizi and his man in the back seat discovered when they tried to jump out; the impact had damaged both doors and neither of them would open.

The driver, next to Zizi, was vainly trying to move the Citroën either forwards or backwards and had not yet real-ized that this was impossible; he was also a little slow on the uptake and couldn't understand why Zizi was shouting at him, in the name of God, to get out of the car.

Thus did the dour taxi-driver prove to be a Fairy God-mother; and by the time a raging Zizi finally managed to extricate himself from the Citroën, followed by the man from the back seat, he found that the third man, who should long ago have given chase, was lying on the sidewalk trying to get air into his lungs, while Julien, ever one to obey orders implicitly, was still inside the hotel as instructed. By this time Marc and Joanna were a good two hundred yards away, unable to believe their luck, but not of a mind of turn around and find out what had caused it.

As Zizi and his sole companion began to give chase the Fairy Godmother again complicated matters by trying to intervene. Doubtless he foresaw, on top of a lost fare, a traffic accident for which he alone would be held responsible. Bulky and enraged, he succeeded in delaying Zizi for a few more seconds.

The result of it all was that Joanna and Marc reached the Boulevard Voltaire at the end of the street with a considerable head start; moreover, they reached it at the very instant that the lights changed at its junction with the Boulevard d'Athènes. Traffic catapulted forward with a roar. The young man and the girl flung themselves in front of this flood of metal and reached the other side. Zizi and his henchmen, arriving while the flood was in full spate, could no more have crossed the street than they could have jumped it.

In front of Joanna and Marc, and a little to their left were the palatial steps leading up to the Gare St Charles. Marc had thought, more or less correctly, that they were being pursued by a car; and any car wishing to reach the railway station had first to turn right into the boulevard (One Way) and then follow a circuitous ramp to the main entrance. He grabbed Joanna's arm and began to haul her up the steps, knowing that not only were they a short cut denied to cars but that at the foot of the last flight they led directly into the bowels of the station: a vast modern booking-hall and the Métro. Vehicles were also denied access to this, and had to arrive and depart on the higher level.

Meanwhile Zizi and his sole remaining aide were making heavy weather of the steps. Both were nearing forty, whereas Marc and Joanna were in their twenties; at such moments the years speak for themselves.

Once inside the booking-hall, Joanna showed signs of flagging, largely due to the huge and delicious meal she had so recently consumed, but Marc grasped her arm, thrust her on to an escalator, and then began to drag her up it, to the surprise and irritation of fellow-travellers who were not in such a hurry. The escalator delivered them into the main concourse.

Here it was again, the recurring motif in the disordered pattern! But the thought barely had time to flit through her mind before she found herself being violently propelled towards one of the platforms. She at once saw why: a train was moving, a guard was blowing his whistle. As they shot past him he made noises of a protesting nature. Marc ignored these and flung himself at the nearest carriage, wrestling with a door; he managed to open it. In a final burst of speed Joanna grabbed the hand-rail, thought for a second that she would surely slip and be crushed between carriage and platform, and then, somehow, found herself in the corridor, turning, catching Marc's outstretched hand and pulling on it. He fell forward on to the floor, feet still bumping along the platform; then doubled himself up and was suddenly, like her, aboard.

Together they grabbed the door and slammed it. Immediately he thrust his head out of the window and looked back. Nobody could conceivably have scrambled on to the train after them, and nobody was even running along the fast-receding platform. The guard was staring in open-mouthed astonishment; then a corner hid him from view.

Marc closed the window and turned back, grinning. 'We made it! I wonder where this thing goes.'

Joanna, still gasping for breath, replied, 'I don't know and I don't care. I just think we should stay on it—to the end of the line.'

FOUR: CAMERA PULLS BACK, REVEALING . . .

1

Zizi, reporting to the penthouse of No. 10 Rue du Palais, stood immobile and dumb while Leo Nogaro raved around the large sitting-room, calling him all the expected names, and a few new ones as well. 'God in heaven! You take *five men* and you can't pick up a couple of half-witted kids!'

Patiently, Zizi explained that one man had been at the back of the hotel on the fire-escape in case the youngsters tried to get out that way. Naturally he had expected Julien and the third man to nab them in the lobby; both were armed, and though they had been instructed not to shoot, sight of the guns should have been enough. However, the boy was a lot more resourceful than expected, and as they knew, the girl had guts. Even so, when they came running out of the hotel Zizi, the man in the back of the car and the driver could easily have intercepted them but for the actions of the taxi-driver.

'You took his number of course.' Leo Nogaro liked to exact retribution from such humble citizens.

No. By the time Zizi returned from the station, out of which the young man and the girl had obviously escaped by Métro, the taxi had reversed down the street and disappeared. The driver had probably found out the provenance of the Citroën and had decided that discretion, even with a lost fare, and considerable damage to pay for, was the better part of valour.

Zizi did not find Little Leo's castigation all that hard to bear; everybody knew that he always blamed other people for all mistakes, even those occasioned by Fate, as in the case of the taxi-driver, or by his own shortcomings. Little Leo. How he hated the nickname which suited him so well! The more so because he was tall, well-built, spectacularly handsome, leaving no doubt in anyone's mind that the 'little' referred to his character or lack of it.

Of course he had his father to thank for this: his father, the man of authority, the self-made man, the big man. Sometimes Leo Nogaro hated his father, yet at the moments of maximum hatred he would often think, 'And what would I have been if he had resembled me?' And thus the moments of maximum hatred were also the moments of maximum respect: even love.

Zizi, though not exactly intelligent, could sense all this, just as he could sense that he too was essential to Leo Nogaro's existence. Here was another reason why he paid little attention to the raving and the rude names; if he had been blaming *himself*, ah, that would have been another matter, but he knew that he had taken all reasonable precautions. Some you win, some you lose.

When the storm had died away, Little Leo opened the door of the bedroom and said, 'By God, you're being slow —what's the matter with you?' This was addressed to a young man called Ahmed who served as both valet and personal bodyguard. Zizi could see that he was packing suitcases, many of them, not with Leo Nogaro's clothing but with the woman's. He knew better than to ask questions; however, the sight gave him food for thought.

Turning back, Leo saw the thought in his lieutenant's eye, and judged that this was the moment to say what had to be said sooner or later: 'My father phoned from Tunis. He'll be arriving at Marignane in about an hour.'

Zizi would have bet any odds that the imminent arrival of Benny Nogaro on one of his extremely rare visits was the real reason for Little Leo's bad temper. More likely than not it was Benny who had ordered the removal of the woman's clothing from the apartment. Had he also ordered his son to pick up the American girl and her young man forthwith? Probably—hence Little Leo's excessive fury at their escape.

In all these deductions he was correct. The telephone call had not been a pleasant one. Leo Nogaro knew that his father no longer trusted his decisions, but never before had this been made so explicit. Naturally he blamed it on the woman. Since he could see that Zizi had already guessed, he said, 'She went to see him.'

Upon consideration Zizi decided that given the circumstances he would have done the same. In his dealings with men Little Leo was known to be unreliable; in his dealings with women he was also, in Zizi's opinion, a fool: though he had never before made quite such a fool of himself as he had over this one; when he grew tired of a woman, and no other had ever held his attention for so long, he became deceitful and dangerous. Aware of the facts, she had gone straight to Benny in Tunis. One had to admire her courage and her sense of priorities.

Neither Zizi nor anyone else employed by Leo knew what it was besides sex which had bound him so strongly to Christina for so long. Something peculiar had happened between a year and eighteen months ago when they had first met. All this business about whether she had or had not been accidentally photographed in Leo's company must have something to do with the past but did nothing to clarify it. In any case Zizi, one of Nature's lackeys by birth and inclination, wasn't interested in clarifying things. People had secrets for their own reasons, good ones usually, and it was foolish as well as dangerous to speculate too much. He thought once again that if only, at the airport, he had reached out and snatched that film from the girl's hands, what a lot of trouble the simple action would have averted.

Leo Nogaro said, 'I'll want four men to come with me when I meet him—separate car. You go to the villa with

Ahmed, see everything's okay.' The Villa Isabelle, incon-
spicuous and impregnable, had been built by Benny Nogaro
on a shoulder of rock overlooking the Corniche: within a
few minutes of the city but sufficiently removed from its
teeming centre. Zizi was pleased to be going there rather
than the airport; he had a feeling that this particular encounter between father and son was not going to be a happy one.
Better, therefore, not to witness it.

2

Joanna's heartfelt wish to stay on the train until the end of
the line (and she had been thinking in terms of Paris or even
Istanbul) was not to be granted. The Ticket Inspector
informed them that they had boarded the 9.58 from Marseille to Nice; only when he mentioned the fare did they
remember their sumptuous meal and what it had cost. Marc
had nothing left but a few francs, and when Joanna had
emptied her purse they were just able to pay for two return
tickets to the first stop, Toulon.

Obviously it wasn't going to be safe to go back to the
Hôtel Métropole-St Charles to collect their possessions;
these would have to be reclaimed at a later date and by
someone else, someone like Marc's 'cousin' and some-time
yachting companion, large Jean-Michel of the Bar des
Moulins, perhaps in the company of a few fellow Rugby
players. Neither were they sure how wise it would be for
them to stay at any other hotel; if their adversary was Leo
Nogaro, and there seemed little doubt about that, then few
hotels in the city would be willing to withold information
concerning their guests. Marc thought that this might be
the moment to call upon Great-aunt Claudine for some secure
hospitality.

So far so good. When the reached Toulon they consulted
a platform timetable and saw that there was a train back to
Marseille at 11.03, only a mere twenty minutes to wait. A

cup of coffee would have been pleasant, but though there
were many cafés near the station they came to the conclusion that they'd better preserve their few francs for the
Métro.

However, when the 11.03 came rolling in, they immediately noticed that there was something curious about it: no
brightly-lit compartments with sleepy faces peering out,
merely shuttered chinks of light here and there. No one
descended; three businessmen climbed aboard. Then they
realized: it was The Blue Train, there were no compartments, only sleeping-cars all the way to Paris.

They ran to the Guard who had admitted the three men.
He glanced at them and at their tickets and shook his head;
the tickets would not have entitled them to so much as a
couchette, even if such low-class accommodation had been
available on The Blue Train, which it wasn't, and even if
they'd been able to pay the humble supplement. Still shaking
his head he climbed aboard, and the train eased itself out
of the station.

Only then did Marc and Joanna discover their true plight.
A booking-clerk, about to close his office, informed them
that the next departure for Marseille-St Charles was at
4.50 a.m. next morning, arriving at 5.49.

Marc said, 'This is ridiculous,' and stormed out of the
station to indulge in an orgy of argument with the only
two taxi-drivers on the rank. It was a mere forty miles to
Marseille, and they would assuredly be paid the other end.
Eighty miles, they replied in unison, at this hour! On the
off-chance of getting their money the other end! Off-chance!
shouted Marc. He would like to have defeated them by
waving Joanna's American Express Card under their noses,
but unfortunately, ever since losing it in London, she always
kept it in her document-case.

What the hell was the matter with them? Or didn't they
want to make money? The younger man said that he was
going home to make love. Marc then called them typical

useless, bone-idle Toulonnais. They called him a typical
Marseille shit-head trying to show off in front of his girl.

Raging, Marc then used a few of their last remaining
francs to telephone Great-aunt Claudine. Joanna said, 'Isn't
it a bit late, eleven-thirty? If she's that old.'

'You don't know her—she never goes to bed before midnight.'

The conversation was remarkably practical and matter-
of-fact amid the surrounding disorder. Certainly he must
come and see her. An American girl, how interesting! Attractive? Never mind, she would wait and see for herself. At
what time? Of course, six a.m. would suit her perfectly, but
they might have to wait for their croissants. Or perhaps
they would prefer a *petit déjeuner anglais*, it was a long time
since Marguerite had prepared one, she would so much
enjoy it. Until then!

Joanna could not quite share this septuagenarian composure. Trying to get comfortable on a hard seat in a chilly
waiting-room, Marc's arm around her, she could only think
what a disaster the whole thing had turned out to be from
its beginning all those days, weeks ago. The realization,
which came to her after a moment's reckoning, that only a
mere thirty-six hours had passed since she'd first become
aware that a silver-grey Mercedes was following her seemed
quite impossible. Was it, could it conceivably have been,
only last night that she had woken up at about this very
hour believing Marc to be capable of all kinds of perfidy?

Time had lost its meaning; without sleep, everything lost
all meaning and proportion. What the hell were they doing,
sitting her at three in the morning like a couple of refugees?
The answer was simple: they *were* a couple of refugees, and
they were probably a lot better off in the station waiting-
room at Toulon than anywhere in Marseille where Monsieur
Leo Nogaro was out gunning for them.

Be thankful for small mercies, Joanna! But this wooden
seat certainly didn't *feel* like a small mercy.

3

Anybody watching the meeting of Monsieur Leo Nogaro
and his father at the airport (and somebody was always
watching them) would have seen a warm Mediterranean
family reunion with hugging and kissing on both cheeks;
indeed, at one level this display was sincere. The experienced
watcher might have noticed a slight hesitation in Little Leo
before he greeted his beautiful mistress in the same way; as
a matter of fact he would have liked to ignore her altogether,
but something about Benny Nogaro's manner warned him
that this would be unwise. They too kissed formally; and
then of course the softness of her and her familiar scent
aroused sensual memories and, cursing inwardly, he desired
her while at the same time feeling that she had betrayed
him by her visit to Tunis.

It had been his intention to drive the two of them in his
Lincoln while the bodyguard followed close behind, but
Benny signalled to one of the men to take the wheel, thus
indicating more clearly than he could have done in words
that he had no intention of saying anything private to his
son until they were alone at the Villa Isabelle. If Leo had
been a little less self-centred, a little less apprehensive, he
would have realized that this was sensible; in any case,
Benny never talked in front of women.

The drive back to the city was awkward, devoted to
meaningless chit-chat, made no easier by the fact that
Christina never opened her mouth; this was particularly
irritating because, like most women and all sophisticated
ones, she was adept at bridging conversational chasms and
shooting emotional rapids. Luckily there was little traffic so
late at night, and the journey was quick.

Only when they were at long last alone together in Benny
Nogaro's study with its magnificent sea view, a low full
moon and racing clouds, shimmering reflections fading and
being reborn, did he say, 'So—you made a cock-up of

grabbing those two youngsters.' He had settled behind his desk as if interviewing some new employee: an intentional gambit of course, nothing he did was ever unintentional. Leo spared a moment to wonder who the hell had slipped this piece of news to him during the few minutes between his leaving his plane and getting into the car. But why bother? He always knew. 'Zizi was in charge. A taxi-driver rammed the car by mistake.'

'Still blaming other people. You should have been there yourself.'

'A stake-out? To pick up a couple of kids?'

'If those kids hold what we think they hold, they're extremely dangerous. And you've lost them.'

'They'll turn up.'

'You had them, Leo, you held them in your hand—it may never happen again. And why don't you sometimes listen to other people? That woman of yours was right, you should have let the girl ship the film to England, nobody would have given it another thought.'

'I disagree. It's a risk we couldn't have taken. If the film shows her, with me . . .' He began to pace about, forgetting how much the habit irritated his father. The moon disappeared behind a cloud, etching its outline in silver. 'Anyway, we may *not* be on it. And even if we are, why should they bother with us?'

'Because you've alerted them, you idiot, and they're not fools. You're in danger, Leo, that's why I'm here. And for God's sake, sit down!'

His son obeyed. The moon reappeared, paving the sea with a glittering path, right up to the terrace.

'Now,' said Benny, 'what the hell did you think you were doing at the airport last night? I've told you a thousand times that people should be killed only as a last resort.'

Leo sighed. Had it been Christina, or some other informer, who had told him about Carlo César? 'It *was* a last resort. He recognized me.'

'What were you doing there? What do you employ other people for?'

'Some things one must do oneself.'

The attempt at integrity fell upon deaf ears. 'Yes, like picking up a boy and girl who may hold your life in their hands. Did you shoot the man yourself?'

'Yes.'

'Don't get a taste for it—you could.'

'I never thought they'd be there at that hour. I wanted to search the office in case he had the film. How was I to know they'd be fucking on a desk?'

His father suddenly brought a large fist crashing down on to the Moroccan blotter in front of him, making an assortment of other objects jump in shock; a vase with a single yellow rose in it fell to the floor. 'Don't talk like a gutter-Arab, you're supposed to be an educated man.' A keen glance. 'Are you smoking khif again?'

'No, Father, I promised.'

Benny eyed him wearily. 'I'm not sure you see the danger even now.'

'It's obvious.'

'Then tell me—what would *you* do if you held that film . . .?' He raised a hand commanding silence. 'And if you and the woman *are* on it?'

Leo smiled. 'Well, that's a little different, I'm your son.'

'There is no *difference*. How many times have I told you that with some part of himself, however small, every man on this earth is a crook. So, what would you do?'

'Use it to get money.'

'From whom?'

'Us, of course.'

Benny Nogaro nodded and sat back in his chair, staring out at the moonlit sea. 'I think I'd better send you on a long, long holiday. I suppose I could bring in Louis Armand from Nice.'

Little Leo was truly thunderstruck by this Olympian

reprimand. 'Why? I mean, why was it wrong, what I said?'

'Foxley,' said his father. 'Charles Foxley. That's why it's wrong.'

Leo's mouth opened slightly.

'Supposing they sold it to him? Can you imagine what *he'd* do with evidence like that—yes, yes, if it exists. And what about that bloody woman of yours? She could blackmail us with it till the end of time. We come third on the list, Leo, a very late third.'

After a pause: 'The kids aren't . . . as clever as you are, they won't know that.'

'Are you God? How do you know who's clever and who isn't?'

Leo spread his hands. He looked, as he felt, utterly bewildered. His father was sorry for him; even loved him for his childish dejection. But perhaps there had been enough sympathy, enough love. He said, 'What reports do you have on their movements?'

'Not many.'

'With the most efficient information network in France, not many.'

'We know they got out of his flat—went to this hotel. Nobody saw them all day, but they were asking questions this evening.'

'What questions? Where?'

'The bar at the bottom of the boulevard for a start. They were trying to find out who lived in the apartment.'

His father became very still, voice soft. 'In your apartment?'

'Yes. The patron's one of ours—he reported it at once.'

'What did they ask him?'

'I just told you, they . . .'

'Exactly what, Leo?'

'Oh, the usual amateur detective stuff. They'd noticed a lot of nice gardens in the area, and . . .'

'Jesus Christ!' said his father, still quietly. 'Don't you see what that means?'

'Naturally they're interested in . . .'

'Interested shit, they *know*, Leo! Why would they ask about your apartment and its garden unless they'd seen it on that damned film?'

4

Marc's Great-aunt Claudine, aged seventy-two, who never went to bed before midnight, was up to welcome them when they arrived at six a.m. She had even seen to her face which had once been beautiful: 'making the best,' as she would often say, 'of a bad job'. She was tall and thin, a little lame with arthritis and therefore bent to one side, but she had even capitalized on this infirmity, using it as part of her stance, making it oddly elegant. Her hair was tied up *à la Créole* in a silk scarf which exactly matched a robe originally created for her by Balenciaga; this, she told Joanna, was a copy made by a clever little woman around the corner; she had, she said, never worn any other peignoir, merely a succession of these copies. 'Why change,' she asked rhetorically, leading them into her salon, 'when that brilliant man made for me the ultimate?' Her English was excellent: from constant reading, Joanna wondered wryly, of the British gutter-press?

She turned to examine them closely in the brilliant morning light, dark eyes vivid and youthful in the lined face. 'You look as if you'd slept in a barn. Ah, youth!'

Marc told her that on the contrary they had failed to sleep in the waiting-room of Toulon railway station.

'I suppose,' said Great-aunt Claudine, a shade doubtfully, 'that even this might be romantic.'

They assured her that it was not.

A mouth-watering scent of grilling bacon was now stealing through the apartment; Marguerite was obviously hard at work in the kitchen on her 'English breakfast'.

Great-aunt Claudine said, 'Will you bath first or will you eat first?'

Joanna replied eagerly, 'The bath, please. I feel . . .' She looked about her at the delicately-coloured room: all gilt and ivory, with pale blue chairs and sofas, in any of which she could have slept for hours: pastel cushions in rose and primrose-yellow and apricot, here and there a choice piece of Louis Quinze, eighteenth-century Sèvres, a Fragonard over the white marble fireplace, a pair of Bouchers on each side of the door. And all this inside one of those shabby old apartment buildings so much loved by the French and so mysteriously secretive to most other nationalities; in the United States the staircase could only have led to a cheap doss-house.

The bathroom was enormous, as were the claw-footed bath and the waiting towels. A soft white robe had been draped over a chair for Joanna's use. Feeling pampered and luxurious, teetering between sleep and hunger, she emerged to find that Marc, having taken a quicker and more bracing shower, was already showing his great-aunt the enlarged photographs of the woman and the two men on the roof.

'Yes, yes,' she was saying, 'the younger Nogaro. So good-looking, but they say he's useless, can't even keep the police in order. But . . .' She picked up a magnifying-glass and examined the three people more closely; then laid a thin and wrinkled finger on the woman. 'I know this face. I can't place it.' She examined it again. 'Yes, most certainly—quite familiar. Dear God, how one's memory disintegrates!'

They ate their breakfast, eggs and bacon and sausage and tomato, watched by its cook, one of those squat French countrywomen who use a grim face to mask their natural good humour. Even her jokes were dour, and could only be identified as such by the infinitesimal smile which accompanied them: as, 'Now look what you've done! The whole place will be covered with newspapers and trashy magazines until she discovers who that woman is.' And indeed Great-aunt Claudine could already be heard rootling about in the small room, at the far end of the apartment, which housed her disreputable library. It seemed that Marguerite kept the stacks of reading-matter until such time as lack of space demanded their eviction to make room for more.

When they'd finished eating the indomitable lady appeared, clutching a dozen copies of the British *News of the World* and said, 'You, Marc, will take your great-uncle's dressing-room, and you, my dear, will use my little spare room. And you will *sleep*.' A severe glance at her great-nephew. 'No delicious tiptoeing along corridors.' It seemed that the kind of behaviour she enjoyed reading about was not countenanced in her own establishment. 'If I were you,' she added to Joanna, 'I'd lock my door. But there, it's much too long since I was young!'

When they had obediently retired to their respective quarters, she looked at Marguerite and said, 'I wondered when he'd fall in love.'

'You think so?'

'Don't be ingenuous, it doesn't suit you.'

'She's so skinny.'

'These days they like them skinny. Come, I have work to do. You may carry *Paris-Match*, you're younger than I am.'

5

Jonathan Heming Duncliffe arrived at Marseille-Marignane from Madrid at nine-ten that same morning, while Joanna and Marc were still asleep. This particular member of Charles Foxley's private intelligence network had intended to approach the South of France from the opposite end of the littoral, but there had been no suitable flight to Nice; moreover, a telephone call had established the fact that Julia, who usually offered him bed in return for board at the town's better restaurants, was in Grenoble and would not be returning until April 26th.

Duncliffe reckoned that if he started his tour at Marseille, where he had excellent contacts, and progressed slowly along the coast in an easterly direction, he could pass the intervening days in some comfort, acquire a tan, arrive in Nice the day after his friend's return, and continue the bed/board relationship thereafter. In any case he felt sure that Foxley was mistaken and that this third visit to the French Riviera within a year would prove as profitless as the other two.

In spite of his appreciation of the creature comforts, Duncliffe was a dedicated professional and loyal to his paymasters. His services had been dispensed with by MI5, on the insistence of the CIA, not because he was lazy or incompetent but because he had worked too hard and thereby learned a great deal too much.

Foxley would not have been surprised to hear that he had reserved a room at the Hôtel Pharo; after all, it was the most expensive in the city. Replying to any such criticism, Duncliffe would have said that it was also the most impersonal; he might possibly have to meet some diverse characters in Marseille. Inspector Brisson of the Central Division, for instance, would feel perfectly at home and uncompromised in the bar of the Pharo. If he proved to be available. He was available. They met in the bar for coffee and cognac at ten-thirty.

Brisson, like Duncliffe himself, was an efficient and ruthless professional; they understood each other perfectly and might have been brothers: under the skin, that is. For whereas Duncliffe was large, fair and blue-eyed, attractive to women in a somewhat raggedy English upper-class manner, Brisson was slim, neat, black-eyed, attractive to women because they were titillated by something dangerous in him.

He said, 'Still the same old business?'

Duncliffe's French was, like his person, English upper-class and raggedy, but fluent. He nodded. 'Got anything for me?'

Brisson smoothed his little black moustache this way and that with a carefully manicured finger. 'Perhaps I'm wrong, but wasn't Leo Nogaro one of your interests?'

Certainly Leo Nogaro was one of Duncliffe's interests, one among many. 'What's he been up to?'

'All the usual things of course, heroin, prostitution, but also . . .' He frowned, examining the immaculate finger-nails.

'But also?'

'I find it hard to express. He has been behaving in a way not . . . typical, granted that he's foolish and inexperienced.' Inspector Brisson went on to describe the murder of Carlo César and his secretary, and the subsequent fire at the office: undoubtedly Nogaro's work, since the device used was identical to that which had burned the Hôtel Perdrix to the ground a year earlier.

'Why a fire? To get rid of the bodies?'

'Apparently not. Things weren't arranged that way. The purpose would seem to have been to destroy some . . . package, cargo, which Monsieur César was handling. Or which Nogaro suspected he might be handling.'

The Inspector then went on to explain that there had been a large American film company in town for six weeks, causing all the usual headaches; they had in fact been staying at this hotel. On the day prior to the fire an American girl, employed by the company, had approached a gendarme on duty at the airport, saying that three men were trying to take from her a couple of metal boxes containing film. The gendarme had naturally made a note of the incident, and an Air France employee had been a witness, but the girl herself never reported it.

At this point Duncliffe decided that perhaps Inspector Brisson was working a little too hard to earn his fee. Leo Nogaro was of interest, *non sequiturs* were not. Brisson probably suspected this, for he added smoothly, 'There is, you see, a connection. The man whom Nogaro killed that same night, whose office he burned, had for six weeks been agent for all film dispatched to England by the company. On top of this it was reported to us that a room here in the Hôtel Pharo had been broken into, searched, ransacked. The room belonged to the same American girl. Again she didn't report the matter.'

He let the implications of this sink in before continuing: 'One of Nogaro's men, known as Zizi Lacombe, was seen out there in the courtyard during the afternoon in question. He may also have been at the airport, we're not sure. But he was certainly present last night when another hotel near the railway station was the scene of . . . some kind of fracas —in that area one can never find witnesses. The same girl had stayed at the hotel the preceding night. With her boyfriend.' He raised a neat hand and gestured.

Duncliffe said nothing, but sat deep in thought, smelling his cognac. 'What you're implying is that there's something connected with the film which Leo Nogaro badly needs to get hold of.'

'Or destroy.'

'Mm! It's an hypothesis, not much more.'

Inspector Brisson again smoothed his moustache. 'It's a little more. You see, on the last few days of filming these people were up at Notre-Dame-de-la-Garde. Leo Nogaro has an apartment just off the Boulevard André Aune, it's overlooked from Notre-Dame. I know this because on certain occasions I myself have taken the opportunity of overlooking it.'

'And it would have been this film which the girl was taking to the airport.'

'Part of it, yes.'

Duncliffe considered the elaboration of the hypothesis in silence. He felt, deep within his stomach, a very faint stirring which could have been excitement. He said, 'Obviously the film was never delivered to this freight agent or Nogaro wouldn't have been pursuing the girl and her boyfriend twenty-four hours later.'

'Agreed.'

'Therefore they're holding on to it. I wonder why.'

'It's the property of their employers, and one presumes that such work is valuable, difficult to replace.'

'You don't think there could be a more . . . personal reason? After all, they must realize that they're sitting on something which is highly important to a rich and powerful man.'

Inspector Brisson smiled, showing perfect teeth. 'These days anything is possible, everyone is wise to every racket —personally I blame it on television. If they're thinking of blackmailing Nogaro . . . I take it that's your meaning?'

Duncliffe nodded.

'They're either very stupid or very clever. Particularly since Benny Nogaro arrived here last night.'

'Doesn't do that very often, does he?'

'Hardly ever these days.' They regarded each other with pleasure, enjoying the interlacing possibilities. Then the Englishman pulled an untidy-looking notebook from his pocket. 'Can you give me the name of the American girl?'

'Joanna Sorensen. Her friend is Marc Gérard. The film, if you're interested, is called *The Sleeping Dog*.'

'And filming is now finished?'

'Only here. It will continue at some studio in England.' He glanced at his watch; then placed on the table between them the folded newspaper he had been holding; these were the usual signs of impending departure.

Duncliffe said, 'Inspector, I realize this is . . . dangerous territory for you, but do you have an informer inside Leo Nogaro's organization?'

'Naturally.'

'If I'm careful, would you allow me to speak to him?'

'I think it could be arranged.'

'As soon as possible?'

'I'll see what I can do. Here?'

'Is this a good place?'

'Why not? What is your room number?' He made a note of it; then excused himself and went to the Men's Room. Duncliffe picked up his newspaper as if to glance at the headlines and, in doing so, slipped a wad of five-thousand-franc notes inside it. Presently Inspector Brisson returned, collecting the paper, he said, 'If you're not in your room I'll leave a message with reception—merely the time.'

'Thank you, Inspector.'

'Thank *you*, Monsieur Duncliffe.'

Following this conversation, Jonathan Duncliffe sat slumped into his chair for ten minutes, staring at the empty brandy-glass. Then he unfolded his large body, left the hotel, and walked along the Corniche, letting a fresh sea-breeze blow through his brain, sweeping it clear of old ideas and suspicions so that he could examine the new idea, new suspicion, more clearly. Then he walked back to the hotel, went to his room and paced up and down it, still unsure. There had been so many false trails, so many dead ends; most of them had initially seemed more promising than this strange rag-bag of circumstances which, if you looked at it closely, didn't seem promising at all. And yet . . . Nogaro.

While he was pacing the telephone rang. Brisson's voice: 'You said as soon as possible.'

'I meant it.'

'Good. Because our friend is on duty from noon until late tonight. He could therefore see you immediately, or not until tomorrow.'

'Immediately.'

'He'll be there in ten, fifteen minutes.'

The man who came into the room a quarter of an hour later was the thickset balding individual who had caused such havoc in the lives of Joanna and Marc: the man whom she had glimpsed in the parking-lot at Notre-Dame and had later failed to recognize at the airport.

It came as no surprise to Duncliffe that this individual was willing to betray his master at a price. Nogaro must indeed be careless or lazy or a bad judge of character; Duncliffe himself would never have employed him in a thousand years, but then his life had depended for its success on many such men; he knew them well; he had never yet met one who commanded either respect or sympathy. Whatever Leo Nogaro and his infamous father might be, they were not this.

He described the whole incident very clearly: how he had driven Monsieur Nogaro and two other men up to Notre-Dame where they were filming: how they'd followed this girl to the airport; how he and the other two had chased her into the terminal while Monsieur Nogaro stayed in the car; but she had run straight to a gendarme and they had been forced to disappear quickly.

When Duncliffe asked him whether he had returned to Marignane later in the day to call on a certain Monsieur Carlo César the visitor paled perceptibly, turning an un-attractive shade of olive-green; no, he knew nothing about that, nothing but what he'd read in the newspaper.

'Were you involved in an incident last night, at an hotel near the Gare St Charles?'

The informer was becoming increasingly uneasy at the extent of his interlocuter's knowledge; yet Inspector Brisson, whom he could trust (at least until the moment when he ceased to be of use and was abandoned for it) had told him that the Englishman was nothing to do with the police. 'Yes, I was at the hotel.'

'What happened?'

Although he himself had been at the back of the place, on the fire-escape, he was able to give an accurate second-hand description of the débâcle at the Hôtel Métropole-St Charles.

'So that the girl and the young man still have . . . whatever it is that Leo Nogaro wants?'

'They must. It wasn't taken from them last night.'

Duncliffe nodded absently and went to the window; the curtains were almost closed even at this hour of the morning; he knew that uncurtained windows worried men like his present visitor, for good reasons. He looked out over the Old Port, but didn't really see it. When he turned back he was holding his wallet between thick capable fingers. He said, 'Answer me this . . .' And to emphasize the importance of the coming question he tapped the wallet lightly against his other hand. '*Why* is Leo Nogaro so keen to get hold of that film?'

Eyes on the wallet, the man regretfully admitted that he had no idea.

Duncliffe tried again. 'You don't know what there is on it that interests him so much?'

The man dragged his eyes away from the wallet with some difficulty.

'Because if that's the case,' said Duncliffe, 'we're simply wasting each other's time.' He was on the point of replacing the wallet when the man said, 'I heard . . . I don't know the truth of it, and in such matters one always wishes to be truthful.'

'Naturally.' The irony sank without trace.

'One of the fellows I work with said it was something to do with a woman.'

'What woman?'

'One of Nogaro's women.'

'I don't understand.'

'Neither do I. But it's possible . . . I mean, Monsieur Nogaro is famous for such things—possibly he's carrying-on with . . . well, the wife of some important man, it wouldn't be the first time. Perhaps with his own father's mistress, who knows? And if he, and she . . .'

'Had been photographed by mistake.'

He spread his hands. 'It's guesswork, Monsieur, it's just a story, there are always stories.'

When he had been paid for his story, and long after he had gone, leaving the smell of garlic and fear and betrayal behind him, Duncliffe stood in the middle of the curtained room, exactly where he had been when the door closed.

From all he had heard, and he'd made it his business to hear a great deal, it would be typical of Leo Nogaro to be having it off with . . . Oh, for God's sake! With the wife of the *préfet* or the mayor: yes, even with his own father's mistress if she happened to be lying around unused. And yet . . .

It was certainly a shot in the dark, but then every single one of those inspired guesses which eventually led to his expulsion from the Secret Service racket had been shots in the dark, they were the hallmark of his trade.

One of the rules was that you never telephoned Foxley at his office. Well, there was said to be an exception to every rule. If this was it, he'd get first prize, and if it wasn't he'd be looking for another job, what the hell!

6

Charles Foxley was, as it happened, chairing the Friday Board Meeting of Maxcom. Since the company all but ran itself and had made a steadily increasing profit for the last nine years, the Board Meeting was always one of the low points of his week and he was glad of an excuse to leave it.

He also appreciated the fact that if Duncliffe, of all people, saw fit to break a rule there would be a good reason for his doing so; therefore he listened with attention to what his man in Marseille had to tell him; then asked, 'Am I to understand you think I ought to come out there?'

Duncliffe wasn't sure; it was possible he'd be wasting his time, particularly in view of the fact that following the incident at the cheap hotel the young American girl and the

Frenchman had disappeared. 'On the other hand,' he added, 'if they suddenly decide to show up, and you aren't here, and other people get to them first . . .'

'That mustn't be allowed to happen. It's a risk I'm not prepared to take.'

'I don't see how we can actually prevent it. Without knowing where they are.'

'Somebody must know.'

'Well, sir, I was thinking—if they're doing the studio work on this film in England, starting in a few days' time, there's got to be a London office. Production office.'

'That's a good idea, I'll see what I can do. What's the film called?'

'*The Sleeping Dog.*'

Foxley made a note of it, and sat staring at the title, lost in thought.

'Hello?'

'Sorry—I'm thinking. Hold on.'

Duncliffe held on for a full minute; then the voice from London said, 'Anything else I ought to know?'

'Yes. Nogaro Senior suddenly turned up here last night. Rare occurrence, could mean Action Stations.'

Evidently this information clinched the matter. 'All right, I'll fly out by the first available plane. My secretary will phone time of arrival.'

As soon as he'd replaced the receiver he summoned his secretary. It didn't take her long to find out what he wanted to know; a single call to *Variety* did the trick. Within five minutes Charles Foxley was talking to the Producer's secretary, Melanie: 'I'm trying to get in touch with a member of your company who I think is still in Marseille. Her name—' glancing at his notes—'is Miss Joanna Sorensen. I wonder if you have a number I can ring?'

Unfortunately not; and he wasn't the only person who wanted to make contact with Joanna Sorensen, Melanie herself was beginning to get a bit desperate. 'But,' she added, 'Jo called me yesterday afternoon, and she promised she'd call again some time today. I'm sure she will, she's very efficient. If you leave your name I'll tell her you're asking for her.'

'My name is Charles Foxley.'

Melanie just managed not to say, '*The* Charles Foxley!'

'If she rings I'd like you to tell her this—to call me, care of Mr Jonathan Duncliffe . . . DUN, have you got that?'

'Yes, Mr Foxley.'

'At the Hôtel Pharo in Marseille. Will you tell her it's *very* urgent.'

'I'll certainly do that, Mr Foxley.'

He next telephoned Kevin in Eaton Square. 'I'll be going away this afternoon for two or three nights.'

Kevin inquired what type of visit it was going to be, sartorially speaking. Foxley told him to pack casual things and a couple of suits, as for a weekend in the country, no golf.

He was surprised to find that he was feeling nothing beyond a vague curiosity; perhaps emotion would come later. He had never doubted what he would do if this contingency ever arose and if it ended in success; doubt lay, as it always had, in his ability to manipulate the circumstances so that they favoured himself and no one else. Often he thought that his emotions were like some kind of bomb, inert, to which the trigger-mechanism would presently be added.

7

Joanna was awakened by Marc sitting on the edge of the bed and shaking her. She wouldn't have minded at all if he had slipped in beside her, but as her brain dragged itself back to full consciousness she realized that he was fully dressed and that his eyes were blazing with another kind of excitement. He kissed her somewhat perfunctorily and said, 'We've found it! We know who the woman is, what the whole thing's about.'

Great-aunt Claudine's salon was barely recognizable. Every chair and table, the piano and most of the floor, were covered in newspapers and magazines. Pieces of headlines and photographs and famous names jumped out at Joanna from every side like naughty children at Halloween: RAPE! BUCKINGHAM PALACE SCANDAL REVEALS . . . ONASSIS. MURDER OF . . . VATICAN. DENIED BY PRINCE. GETTY. SADIST'S VICTIM TIED TO . . . LIZ TELLS ALL. SUICIDE PACT IN STAR'S LUXURY . . . KENNEDY. . . . OF TOP MODEL. HEROIN. VICE-KING TRAPPED AS . . .

Marc had certainly not exaggerated his great-aunt's taste in literature nor the avidity with which she gratified it. She herself, still wearing the Balenciaga copy, headscarf now slightly askew, was on her hands and knees amid the chaos. Joanna noticed that the time was a little after one o'clock, so this had been going on for some five hours. Marguerite, a look of long-suffering patience on her face, deposited a tray with cups and coffee on top of EARL AND TEENAGER IN COURT, sniffed superciliously, and withdrew.

Great-aunt Claudine glanced up at Joanna, asked her to pour the coffee, then pulled one of the enlarged photographs from beneath SEX MANIAC CONFESSES and tapped the woman's face triumphantly. 'Dead. Her body was found in February.'

Joanna gaped. Marc said, 'Exactly.'

His great-aunt thrust out a copy of *Paris-Match*. On the open page was a picture of the same woman: with blonde hair but undoubtedly the same. She was sitting outside a café in bright sunshine and was just raising a hand to hide her face from the camera. Marc took the magazine and translated the caption: 'Last known photograph of Melissa Foxley, taken in Rome by papparazze Ugo Bellini two days before her disappearance.' And the text:

The body of Melissa Foxley, wife of British millionaire Charles Foxley, was found on Monday by two boys playing beside a lake near Penzberg, forty miles from Munich. Mild weather has caused an early thaw in the area.

Munich police have stated that the lake has been frozen to an unknown depth all winter; this makes it difficult to assess with accuracy the exact date of Madame Foxley's death, but what remains of her clothing suggests that she was dressed for a warm day, so she may well have died as late as the end of October last year when Northern Europe experienced an Indian Summer.

Monsieur Foxley flew at once to Munich and has positively identified the body as that of his wife. German officials praised his courage in the face of such a terrible ordeal.

The questions which confront the police of more than one country are these. Where was Madame Foxley between April of last year, when she disappeared, and late October when, if our supposition is correct, she may have died? More importantly, if she was alive in *May* of last year, as now seems certain, why didn't her captors produce her at the time of the ransom demand which Monsieur Foxley was ready, indeed eager, to pay in full?

There followed a reference to a previous edition of *Paris-Match* for the May in question; if Marguerite, to Great-aunt Claudine's fury, had not thrown this away it would doubtless have explained the ransom and its outcome. However, the indomitable old lady had excavated other sources from the litter. Something called *Open File*, which sported on its cover a lady in a diaphanous nightdress, lying on a leopard-skin rug with her throat cut, read as follows: 'The file is certainly still open on the fate of beauteous Melissa, wife of multi-millionaire Charles Foxley, found dead last month in a Bavarian lake.'

Beneath this was a particularly unpleasant photograph

of the body, or what remained of it, shortly after it had been removed from the water.

Melissa, whose previous husband was oil tycoon Nikki Theoradis, disappeared from Rome in May last year. At the time Mr Foxley stated to the Press, 'She has a lot of friends and is probably visiting one of them,' thus suggesting that his wife wasn't in the habit of telling him much about her plans. As for her 'many friends', the late Mr Theoradis could have warned Mr Foxley about *them*. Readers of *Open File* will remember that he all but cut Melissa out of his will, and with good reason. Much to her fury and to the delight of the Theoradis children by his first two marriages . . .

Great-aunt Claudine cried out, 'No, no—that's all vulgar rubbish. Read her this.' It was a full-page spread in *France-Dimanche*, dated May of the year before.

Yesterday, British millionaire-financier Charles Foxley was not at home to the media besieging his twenty-roomed country mansion, Prior's Hill, near Buckland Newton in Dorset, England, but a member of his staff made a statement confirming that a demand had been received for the ransom of his wife, Melissa, famous beauty and jet-set hostess. The spokesman would not name a figure or say in what form the demand had been made, merely that it had come from Europe and that Mr Foxley would be leaving Britain privately within the next twenty-four hours.

British police were asking Pressmen not to prejudice the success of the ransom agreement by making wild guesses and inventing stories. Mrs Foxley's safety might depend on their discretion.

Melissa Foxley, previously Madame Theoradis, vanished from Rome three weeks ago. She and her husband

were staying with a friend, the Principessa Orlani-
Tedesco, at her palazzo outside the city. Mrs Foxley was
last seen, by friends with whom she had lunched, entering
a boutique near the foot of the Spanish Steps. However,
the owner of the shop, Signora Bianca, said that Mrs
Foxley, a well-known client, had not visited her establishment that day, nor indeed for the past week.

Servants at the Palazzo Orlani hinted that Mr and Mrs
Foxley were not on good terms and said that arguments
had been heard. At the time the gutter press of several
countries suggested that Mrs Foxley might well have been
murdered. She was, on the day of her disappearance,
wearing jewellery worth thousands of dollars. These ru-
mours have persisted up to the present time, but have
been silenced once and for all by the ransom demand.

It is not known whether her kidnappers are members
of the Italian underworld or political terrorists such as
the Red Brigade; both groups have committed similar
outrages within the past few months.

Joanna, her brain reeling, said, 'You mean, he *paid* the
ransom?'

'No, he didn't.'

'Because,' added Great-aunt Claudine, 'when he arrived
at the rendezvous in Milan she wasn't there.'

'And neither were the kidnappers.'

Joanna sat down, first clearing away piled copies of the
News of the World. 'So what went on?'

'Nobody knows.' He picked up *Open File* again and handed
it to her. The paragraph, marked with thick black pencil,
read:

Questions, Questions! What *did* happen in Milan when
billionaire Charles Foxley went there prepared to pay an
estimated million and a half dollars for the return of his
wife, Melissa? Why didn't the kidnappers show? Why

was there no word from them or from Melissa? Why, if nobody intended to collect the loot, did they take the trouble to demand it? And where *is* Melissa? Maybe all those stories about her being dead are true. Very much an Open File, readers. Don't forget to order next week's edition!

Joanna threw this aside impatiently. 'It doesn't make sense.'

'Nothing makes sense,' said Marc. 'We took a picture last Wednesday of a woman who died seven months ago.'

'The ransom story—it wasn't just a Press invention?'

'Oh no.' Great-aunt Claudine reached for a copy of *Figaro*. 'It was in all the papers.' She found the page and read, 'Monsieur Foxley returned to London yesterday, heart-broken. "It is terrible," he said, "to have one's hopes raised, only for them to be broken like this. If it was . . ." *Une farce?*'

Marc said, 'Hoax.'

'Extraordinary language! "If it was a hoax it was a very cruel and vicious one. I don't understand it."'

'He can say that again!'

'But you see,' said Marc, eyes shining, 'why they don't want anyone to get hold of that film.'

'I can kind of see why *she* wouldn't, but where does this crook Nogaro fit in?'

'Where's that gossip column, the British one?'

His great-aunt handed it to him. 'This was in April last year, before she disappeared, before they went to Rome. "What *would* we do without Mrs Charles Foxley, the lovely Melissa, to keep us guessing? A couple of months ago it was luscious John Lasenbury Junior, Newport's Number One, holding her up (closely) on the ski-slopes at Gstaad. But at last night's opening of Clements, the Apple's latest swing-in, there she was tête-à-tête (very) with Claudio Bassani, *said* to be engaged to a certain angry lady from Athens. You've got to hand it to Melissa, she certainly gets around. Lord Ellenby's punch-up at Annabel's, Sven Gaard making a fool of himself at Wimbledon, and was that Leo Nogaro squiring her at baccarat in Cannes? (I'm sure she won!) . . ."' He stopped and looked up at her. 'There's your connection.'

'Doesn't prove much.'

'It proves she knew him pretty well.'

'She knew half the men in Europe pretty well.'

'To me,' said Great-aunt Claudine, the expert in such matters, 'the mystery is this. If your photograph is really of Mrs Foxley, and she is therefore alive, why did her husband identify that body in Germany?'

Joanna shuddered, 'It was in pretty terrible condition.'

'Then he would have said he was unsure, unable to tell. But he didn't, he identified it positively—all the reports we have read state this.'

Marc shrugged. 'He could simply have made a mistake.' It was an aspect of the situation which obviously didn't interest him; he would have done well to pay more attention to his great-aunt who was shaking her head in disagreement. 'No. Everything about Mr Charles Foxley tells me he is a man who does not make mistakes.'

Joanna said, 'I'm not so sure. After all, he married the beauteous Melissa.'

8

The beauteous Melissa, Foxley, ex-Theoradis, also known as Christina Neff, also known as Melinda Grey, born Millicent Ponsonby, was reclining on her bed behind a locked door at Benny Nogaro's Villa Isabelle. She was doing her nails, listening to the voices of Nogaro and Son raised in heated argument, and assessing the possible effect of the argument upon her own fortunes. She had spent much of her life since the age of twelve assessing the effect of other people's arguments upon her own fortunes.

Only the most perceptive sociologist, and sociologists are notoriously blind, would have been able to recognize this woman as a perfect example of the mess which the ludicrous (and by no means defunct, as some suppose) English class system can make of the English. Millicent Ponsonby was born into a typical, well-to-do, middle-class family; they lived in a large house in London's stockbroker belt, and her father owned a factory which made some mysterious component necessary to British Industry. But British Industry was then in a state of rapid decline, and need for the Ponsonby component soon dried up completely.

By the time Millicent was old enough to be accepted by one of the 'right' private schools her father could no longer afford its fees, though he struggled gamely to pay them. The overheard conversations of those years ensured that the small girl grew up with a lasting sense of insecurity, feeling herself to be a crushing burden to the only person in the world she was ever to love.

When her father's business collapsed she at first suffered bitterly on his account, and later more bitterly on her own, for she was thrust, with parental apologies, into a fearful Comprehensive School, not far from the ugly little flat which was all her father could now afford. Then began the years of utter misery which were to mould her character for ever; nobody in this alien land would ever speak to her unless they wished to mock her 'posh' accent; naturally she learned nothing, but, in her desire for some kind of acceptance, was forced to run the gauntlet of every obtainable drug; however, she at least managed to avoid the customary gang-rape by driving a chisel into the ringleader's private parts. Foolish of them to have chosen the woodwork classroom!

Comprehensive School may have given her no academic education but it had educated her quite efficiently in the ways of the street which are the ways of the world. When she was sixteen her father, who had taken to the bottle, killed himself in a car crash. Dreams of this were to haunt her for the rest of her life. Her mother, inclined to be bossy when affluent, had by then turned into a snivelling frump, endlessly whining about 'the good old days'.

Escape was clearly essential, but nine years of education had left young Millicent with only two attributes: her beauty (outstanding) and her secretarial ability (negligible); she could therefore become a secretary or a whore. She chose the former, and was introduced by the boss's randy son to an interesting variation of the latter in the shape of her first visit to a London nightclub. Dotted about the dimly-lit room were a number of attractive girls; these, whose only duty, it seemed, was to be all things to all men, were known as 'hostesses'; further inquiry elicited the information that they were not expected to sleep with the 'punters', many of whom were too old or too drunk for such activity anyway, but might do so if they desired.

Millicent Ponsonby changed her name to Melinda Grey and joined their ranks. The clubs in which she then worked were the proper University with which to follow a Comprehensive School. As things turned out, she slept with a great number of clients; but she was *not* a nymphomaniac, and nearly blinded the girl who had been foolish enough to suggest she was. By the time she was eighteen there was little she didn't know about men, and nothing she didn't know about her own ambitions. These were based upon a simple premise: never, but never, would she again be thrown out of her own world into the world of the Comprehensive, and the only way to ensure it was Money.

Several of the 'hostesses' had married wealthy punters: from sleazy club to rich respectability in one bound. Millicent/Melinda was too canny for such overt behaviour (after all, she was a 'lady'), and therefore became determined to meet her rich man outside the tainted enclave. It took a little time and thought, but she finally nabbed Nikki Theoradis at St Tropez where she was holidaying with a trusted colleague.

Theoradis was at that time sixty-seven years old. Millicent/Melinda, who now changed her name to Melissa, realized that she would have to submit to his embraces, but never in her wildest dreams did she imagine that the old goat would actually be jealous. For God's sake, she was now surrounded by hordes of lovely young men, what did he expect?

Nikki Theoradis was no full-blooded, up-and-at-your throat Greek; he was a fastidious elderly playboy, in many ways disgusted with himself for wishing to add this beautiful nineteen-year-old to his collection of treasures. Millicent/ Melinda/Melissa, disporting herself among the male *jeunesse dorée*, as well as with this carefully chosen ski-instructor or that irresistible member of a yacht's crew, thought she was being discreet; in fact, not one of her escapades was overlooked by her aged husband, who even employed a private detective to count them. He took note of each; he brooded over each; but never in a thousand years would he have divorced her; the fool he had made of himself through marriage would be nothing to the fool he would appear in the divorce courts; and there were other ways, as Millicent/ Melinda/Melissa discovered when his old enemy, cancer, finally killed him.

His last will and testament was a turning-point in her life; she was twenty-three, she was the fascinating Madame Theoradis, and she was penniless. The chosen world had been snatched away from her once more; once more she was at the mercy of the Comprehensive. It was now that she became obsessed, manically obsessed, by the interlocking ideas of money and freedom.

Sale of her jewellery, reinforced by a number of hard-earned 'gifts', kept her going for three awkward years, but not at all in the style to which she had become accustomed. In some ways this was a blessing in disguise, since at all costs she had to avoid the Theoradis milieu where no rich man would have touched her with the butt-end of a barge-pole, knowing what they did. Never mind! There were other

worlds, there must be other worlds, but where were they
and how did one enter them?

She was not far from the end of her tether when she espied
in the far distance, surrounded by extraordinary objects
such as boardrooms and trout streams and golf-courses, the
dim figure of Charles Foxley attired in sober tweed; he had
no knowledge whatever of yachts, cocaine, private islands,
ski-instructors; indeed, he despised such frippery. Within
six months Millicent/Melinda/Melissa had landed him in
marriage. She was now twenty-eight, as beautiful as ever
and very much wiser. One of her first gambits had been a
'frank' confession of some of her previous stupidities. Foxley
had been touched, but then he was head over heels in love
with her, much to his own surprise.

Perhaps she had really meant to be a dutiful wife; perhaps
she had imagined that she could be faithful to this man,
however dry and unsatisfactory he was as a lover; perhaps it
was only now that she realized how right a certain nightclub
hostess had been about her all those years ago: realized that
her desire for new men was, or had become, an addiction
every bit as compulsive as, say, the lust for heroin.

But Foxley was no Theoradis; whereas the hot-blooded
Mediterranean male had bided his time in silence, the
cold-blooded Englishman had burst out in passionate re-
crimination: on and on, again and again: until at last she
had screamed at him, 'All right then, get rid of me, give me
grounds for divorce.' At which Charles Foxley had shown
the true steel of which he was made: 'Give *you* grounds! And
pay you alimony! Never!' And she knew him well enough
by then to realize that 'never' meant just that. She was
trapped.

She was trapped, but on the other hand his refusal, as
she saw it, gave her permission to do exactly as she wished;
if the mean bastard wouldn't release her, what could be
expect? Mrs Charles Foxley's behaviour now became too
much for all but the most muck-raking of columnists, and

if she was accepted by anyone of consequence, such as the Principessa Orlani-Tedesco, it was only because they felt sorry for Charles Foxley. Moreover, it wasn't only men that she flung in her husband's face; there was more than one drunken scandal; there was a drug-party which ended in a suicide attempt from which she was lucky to have recovered; but the luck, no less than the recovery, did not lead her to sober reflection, only to further excess, so that some of her acquaintances began to wonder whether she wasn't a little mad.

The perspicacious and imaginary sociologist, with his psychiatric box of tricks, might have been able to trace a direct line from the anguished and terrified fourteen-year-old, cringing in a corner on her first day at that Comprehensive School, to this utterly self-absorbed, utterly amoral woman of thirty-three. Nobody else would have cared, even if they'd known the facts.

When Charles Foxley tried to put an end to her disgraceful behaviour he was met with the old demand: he could buy his release with alimony, that was all she asked for: enough money to live the kind of life she wanted, must have, and blessed freedom to go with it.

Never. Why did he refuse when he could so easily have afforded it and when all he got from her was further suffering? There could have been only one answer and it was forever hidden from her because she didn't know, had never known except in regard to her father, the meaning of the word 'love'.

And so it was that the idea had come to her one night when she was lying in bed, high on cocaine, with Leo Nogaro, currently the most attractive and satisfying male she had ever known (and a gangster too, something new, titillating): if her boring, frigid prick of a husband was too mean to divorce her, were there not other ways of getting the necessary money out of him, other ways of escape . . .

She finished her nails and stared at them reflectively,

examining the hands for telltale signs of age. None as yet.

There was silence now. The Nogaros had finished their argument. Leo would be sulking. What, she wondered, would Benny be doing?

Benny was sitting at his desk, lost in thought. He had only just arrived at full comprehension of the extent to which Leo had allowed the Marseille organization to decay and collapse. It appeared that there was no longer any information network worth the name; nobody had even photographed the American girl and the young Frenchman, though there had been at least three opportunities to do so; without photographs for identification, how could anyone be expected to trace them?

He was now sure that Leo would have to go; some harmless job must be found for him under the direction of an old-timer who could teach him all the things which his father had supposed he was absorbing during his apprenticeship: when in reality all he had been absorbing was a taste for money and beautiful women and soft drugs.

Benny Nogaro had not made his empire a model of its kind by being unable to face unpleasant facts; therefore he admitted to himself that under present circumstances there was only a slim chance of finding the young man and the girl, and thus the damnable piece of film which was their evidence. His best hope, and in this Little Leo had been right, but for the wrong reasons of course, lay in the possibility that the two of them would come to *him*, hoping to barter the film for a large sum of money.

But this in itself, if it ever happened, presented new difficulties; because even though he would then hold the evidence he would still be saddled with the unpleasant, because dangerous, business of killing them. With or without the film, they knew too much and would remain a poisonous thorn in his flesh. Nevertheless 'accidents', however well contrived, always led to questions: and the girl was an American citizen, so her Consulate would be stung into convulsive action. The last thing Benny could afford at this moment, with his empire in a state of total disorganization and its army in disarray, was a full-scale inquiry linking the name Nogaro with more murders. Yet in the case of the boy and girl murder would have to be committed, no doubt about that.

He acknowledged that all this was his own fault. He had made the mistake of thinking that after fifty-eight years of hard work (his criminal career had started at the age of six) he deserved a rest; he should have realized that for a man like himself there was no rest short of the grave. In addition, foolish fatherly pride had tricked him into believing that his beautiful boy was a tough chip off the old block, when in fact he took after his mother and was nothing but a soft slice off the old melon. If anything was going to be saved from this mess he, Benny Nogaro, was going to have to save it.

Leo was sulking, not only because his father had at last discovered the extent of his inefficiency and self-deception but because Christina, the previous night, had locked the door of her bedroom against him, refusing to open it. The anger was compounded by his having pretended to himself that he no longer desired her anyway. In the morning, over coffee and croissants, she revealed her reason for denying him access, and anger was compounded all over again. With the utmost dispassion she informed him, in front of his father, that the two of them had made a deal: she would have no more to do with him if Benny would get her, and by inference Leo himself, out of this mess concerning the film. Ignominy was thus crowned by the knowledge that he was no more than a counter on a gaming-table, and one which neither of these expert gamblers valued very highly.

While Benny Nogaro was devising ways to trap Joanna and Marc if they ever broke cover, Charles Foxley arrived at Marignane where he was met by Duncliffe. He immediately asked whether the American girl had yet tried to contact him at the Hôtel Pharo. No, she had not. All they could therefore do was to go straight back to the hotel and wait until she did.

Duncliffe had only met his employer twice before, and had gained an impression of a cold man, even a dull one; nothing he now saw or heard altered that opinion. He himself was gripped by a hunch, a gut-feeling, that they were on to something really important, and though he was not given to pointless enthusiasm, Foxley's utter lack of excitement, after a whole year of searching every corner of the world, seemed to him altogether too dispassionate: not to mention something of a personal put-down. But then, as he drove the man back to Marseille, he became attuned to something else. It took him a little time, even with his acute perception of other people's emotions, to understand that he was in the presence of a tension so great that it could almost be heard, thrumming above the sound of the car's engine.

Self-control was a quality which his dangerous life had taught him to admire, but it had also taught him that if self-control is too rigidly applied the inevitable crisis, when it comes, may well attain hysterical proportions. He began to arm himself against the possible contingency; men in such a condition had been known to run amok, and he had no wish to find himself responsible for a compromised, perhaps even an imprisoned, multi-millionaire.

He also thought, grimly, that if the Sorensen girl did not telephone the London production office, or if she did telephone and the secretary forgot to mention Foxley's message, or if the message didn't interest her, a lot of ifs, then there was no reason why he and Charles Foxley should not sit in the Hôtel Pharo for the next three days, maybe longer, waiting for a contact which was never going to be made.

Meanwhile Joanna and Marc, the objects of all this planning, plotting, surmise, were arguing furiously in Great-aunt Claudine's beautiful salon, now tidied and restored to its former elegance. Their hostess had gone out to have her hair done, and Marguerite's English was rudimentary; they were therefore able to let themselves go.

The revelation that the woman in their photograph had been, still was, Mrs Charles Foxley had boosted Marc to new heights of avaricious optimism, completely unaffected by any feminine caution. If Joanna had found his old posture irritating she found the new one maddening beyond words. 'For God's sake *use your brain*! You can't take on those kind of people, they'll mince you and make hamburgers out of you.'

'While we hold that film? Use your own brain!'

'Look—you may want to have your fingernails pulled out one by one and cigarettes stubbed out on your balls, but I'm not . . .'

'You're still talking about Leo Nogaro—I don't give a damn about him, I'm aiming for Charles Foxley.'

Joanna stared at him, dumbfounded. 'I . . . I guess I didn't hear that correctly.'

'I think you did.'

'But that's *really* immoral, that *is* blackmail.'

'No, please, not again!'

'Nogaro was one thing, he's a crook, he's a killer . . .'

'And Foxley's a multi-millionaire, what's the difference?'

'The *difference*! He's innocent, Marc, he's just like you and me. I'm not having any part of this.' She swung away from him, but he caught her arm as he had done outside the railway station and pulled her back to face him. 'Isn't it about time you got all this moral bullshit straight? Nogaro or Foxley, *our* behaviour's the same. Nogaro or Foxley, it's *our* behaviour you seem to find so immoral—so what's changed?'

'Jesus! I said that from the start.'

'But it hasn't stopped you tagging along. At least I'm not a hypocrite.'

'Hypocrite, me!'

But his face had lit up with a new idea. 'And what about

the beauteous Melissa? I bet *she*'s got a few francs to rub together. Who do you think will make the highest bid?'

Joanna gave him a cold glare. 'Well, I'm sure glad I found all this out now and not later.'

'What?'

'You're a crook yourself. You haven't got the moral sense of a . . . of a coyote.'

'So you think she acted morally!'

'I'm not talking about her, I'm talking about her wretched husband.'

'Okay. You show me *one* self-made man who's never done anything crooked and I'll drop the whole thing.'

Chance plays strange tricks, because it was this remark, in her opinion as stupid as it was base, which made Joanna dissociate herself (as she imagined) from the whole perilous enterprise. In order to remind him that she was an ordinary adult human being with adult standards and a job in the real world outside his half-baked, evil dream, she said, 'I promised I'd call Melanie at the Production Office—would your great-aunt mind?', thus delivering herself, tied and bound, into the hands of his megalomania.

An airy wave of the hand gave her permission to do whatever mundane thing she desired; while she dialled and re-dialled, and re-dialled again, cursing the European and particularly the British telephone system, he retired into the half-baked dream; and it wasn't until he heard her saying, 'Foxley? Melanie, are you sure?' that he snapped back to the here and now, all ears.

'But . . . It's a lousy line—did you say the Pharo? What's he doing . . .?' Only then did she notice Marc's avid expression, and only then realize that her surprise had betrayed her.

Melanie was explaining how Customs clearance had now been negotiated; the two reels could be dispatched tomorrow morning, or even tonight. Joanna, eyes fixed on Marc's eyes, barely heard her, barely knew what she herself replied.

He pounced as soon as she replaced the receiver: 'Foxley's here, at the Pharo?'

No good denying it now. 'He . . . wants me to get in touch with him. Marc, can't you see the danger? How did he find *out?*'

'Money,' said Marc. 'Money, money, money—it's the miracle-worker. You're an American, you ought to know.'

'*Please listen to me!* I love you, I want you to be alive, with *me!*'

'Of course. Where shall we go first, how about the Himalayas?' He took the telephone receiver out of her hand, depressed the button and began to dial. She knew the number by heart; hadn't she lived there herself for two months?

'Marc, think first. Just *think!*'

'I've thought. I've been thinking for three days.'

As the number began to ring she reached forward and pressed down the receiver-rest, cutting the connection. She was really angry now. 'For Christ's sake, what's all this business about money? Nobody needs it that badly.'

'Everybody needs it.' He took her wrist and dragged her fingers away. With the other hand he began to dial again.

'You really *are* a peasant, aren't you?'

'I told you I was.'

The pressure of his fingers had relaxed. She whipped her hand away and cut the connection again. 'A dumb, greedy, stupid peasant who can't see further than the end of his nose.'

She had never known the pale eyes so changed, so hard and metallic. 'Is that better or worse than being a stupid middle-class American who thinks she can make the world's best films?'

They glared at each other for a second. Then Joanna shouted, 'Fuck you, dumb asshole!'

'And fuck you too, Mademoiselle!' This time he didn't bother with her hand but gave her a hard push which toppled her backwards into an armchair. She turned her head away and only heard the whirring sound of the dial; then, 'Hello, Hôtel Pharo? Mr Foxley, please. No, I don't know the room number.'

Joanna found to her fury that she was biting the back of her hand like a child; and like a child, tears of rage were pressing at her closed eyelids.

Marc said, 'Monsieur Foxley? I'm speaking for Joanna Sorensen, you wanted her to call you.'

In the hotel suite Duncliffe picked up the bedroom telephone extension.

Foxley said, 'I take it you're her young French friend.'

'Correct.'

'It's been brought to my attention that you may have in your possession some film which . . . which could be of interest to me.'

'Yes, we have.'

In the bedroom Duncliffe nodded to himself, aware of a strange mixture of emotions, satisfaction and misgiving; being proved right had landed him in trouble before. But, by God, how rarely that feeling in the gut had ever let him down! He glanced through the open door at Charles Foxley and saw the same composed face, the same merciless self-control. He was saying, 'Monsieur Gérard, that is your name . . .?'

His knowledge took Marc aback; he almost at that moment sensed something of the danger against which Joanna had warned him. How did such men learn one's name? 'Yes.'

'This isn't a matter which we should discuss any further on the telephone. We must meet.'

'By all means.'

'However, in order not to waste your time or mine, I . . . I must ask you what the film shows.'

Duncliffe found himself holding his breath. On the other side of the city Joanna held hers.

'The actual film shows very little, but certain frames have been enlarged. They show your wife.'

Silence. Was this, Duncliffe wondered, the moment? Would he break now? No, absolutely not, but the silence was eloquent. Eventually, 'You may come here if you wish.'

'I think,' said Marc, 'I'd be extremely stupid if I did.'

'Not at all. But it's up to you, where do you suggest?'

'The Museum of Fine Arts at the Palais de Longchamp. Do you know it?'

'No, but I'm sure it's easily found.'

'There are two museums, one on each side of the central fountains. Fine Arts is the one on the left. I'll be in the Daumier room on the first floor at three forty-five, an hour from now. And Mr Foxley, please come alone or the deal's off.'

Charles Foxley repeated the instructions, at the same time glancing at Duncliffe to see if he was writing them down. He was.

Marc said, 'I won't be bringing the evidence, not yet.'

'I understand. You'll oblige me, however, by bringing Miss Sorensen—she's my only assurance that I'm not talking to some confidence-trickster. I wasn't born yesterday, Monsieur Gérard.'

'Okay. We'll both be there.'

As soon as he replaced the receiver Joanna said, 'I'm not going, and that's final.' Moreover, she really meant it.

He stared at her; then sighed and shook his head. 'Jeanne, why do you think I want this money?' And, before she could reply: 'For you. For your first film.'

He might as well have hit her with a sledgehammer: *and* below the belt. She gasped, gaped, gasped again; then shouted, 'You bastard! You two-faced crooked *bastard*!' and burst into tears.

FIVE: TRACKING-SHOT TOWARDS
BAR DES MOULINS

1

Great-aunt Claudine did not drive or possess a car; when
she wished to move about in comfort she commanded the
presence of an elderly gentleman called Henri who drove
an elderly Peugeot. She imagined him to belong to a car-hire
firm, but he had long ago retired from this employment and
only acted as her chauffeur because her deceased husband
had once been his commanding officer in the Army, and
because he admired Great-aunt Claudine as a relic of an
older and better world. She paid him perhaps one quarter
of the fare which would have been asked by any ordinary
taxi, but since she never used any ordinary taxi she didn't
know this, and Henri didn't need the money anyway, being
in receipt of a pension which covered all his meagre needs.
He was, needless to say, absolutely reliable, loyal and discreet.

It was this Henri who drove Joanna and Marc, extremely
slowly, to the Palais de Longchamp. He wondered why they
were so silent, heads obstinately averted from each other.
Some lover's tiff no doubt. Ah, youth!

The water-palace, an exceptional concoction of staircases
and arches and colonnades, of statues, cascades, fountains
and more statues, surmounted by some deity escorted by
dripping ladies with large bosoms, was normally one of
Joanna's favourite sights; but as she approached it on this
occasion, not even the curious pagoda-like tower under
which the god was ensconced gave her the slightest pleasure:
it was just another example of the way false and amoral old

Europe charmed you into accepting her on her own shoddy terms.

She longed to be back home in the States where, she told herself, blackmailing lovers like Marc simply didn't exist (imagine Barney conning her into an enterprise like this!) and where values were constant and viable, not, as here, forever changing shape or disappearing altogether. Her anger was compounded by the fact that she knew very well she should have persisted in her refusal to accompany him. Did her very presence here make her the hypocrite he had so unforgivably called her? God in heaven, Europe could turn even ambition into some kind of a crime!

At about the time that they reached the Museum of Fine Arts, Benny Nogaro at the Villa Isabelle was searching their baggage, brought from the Hôtel Métropole-St Charles where it had been lying unclaimed. His examination, more thorough than that made by Zizi, led him to discover Marc's address-book. Quite a find! Particularly as he had now discovered that among the many things Little Leo had allowed to lapse was the invaluable police connection upon which his father had always relied.

So, even if there were no photographs of the couple with which to identify them, and even if certain members of the police force could no longer be relied upon to help trace them, and even if thorough cross-examination of all the hotels had failed to reveal any sign of them, he at least held in his hand a list, with telephone numbers, of all Marc Gérard's friends and relatives. If the young man and the girl weren't staying in a hotel, then they had very likely taken refuge with one of these. But even as he made arrangements to check each of them, beginning with those who were self-evidently members of Marc's extensive family, the situation was in the process of undergoing drastic change.

The Nogaros' luck had by no means run out, as events were swiftly to prove, but owing to Leo's intransigence it was running a little late.

Joanna and Marc had not been examining Monsieur Daumier's work for more than three minutes before Charles Foxley joined them. He was alone. Mutual recognition was immediate.

There were some fifteen other people scattered about the first floor, so they were able to talk with ease while appearing to examine statues and drawings. Foxley assessed his antagonists with his cold greenish eyes, noting their youth, the boy's air of uneasy determination, the girl's air, unmistakable, of wishing she was somewhere else, anywhere else. He had taken a packet of cigarettes and a lighter from his pocket, but now grimaced at them and said, 'I don't suppose one's allowed to smoke in here.'

Marc said that this was so.

'Very well. Let's not beat about the bush. You want me to pay for these photographs of my wife.'

'Yes.'

'How much?'

'A million and a half dollars.'

Foxley's expression did not change; Joanna's revealed incredulous disbelief. Marc added, 'I think they're worth that to you.'

'*Why* do you think so?'

The younger man glanced away from the ice-green stare. He wasn't sure of the answer, but could sense its rightness. 'Because she wants you to think she's dead. Because that was the original ransom demand.'

'Which I never paid.'

'But you were willing to pay it. Somewhere along the line you were tricked, and this photograph's the proof.'

'When was it taken?'

'Three days ago.'

'How am I to believe that? People were always photographing my wife. How am I to know this isn't an old picture, re-hashed, re-touched?'

'The film *proves* it isn't. You get the film too.'

'You're offering to sell me evidence which isn't even your property.'

'That's right. If you find it immoral, other people won't be so choosey.'

'What other people, Monsieur Gérard?'

'Leo Nogaro. The lady herself.'

Charles Foxley nodded; then glanced at Joanna. 'And you, Miss Sorensen, what do *you* think of this . . . transaction?'

'I . . .' She glanced at the young man, a girl so obviously divided that Foxley perceived it at once. He even guessed that affection was possibly pulling her one way, and fear, or even an innate honesty, was pulling her the other. He was not to know about her ambition, but nobody could have missed the anger behind her reply: 'I hate the whole goddam thing, but . . .' Again she looked at the boy and then away. 'But I'll go along with Marc because I . . . guess I have to.'

'I see.' And to the young man, 'Naturally I must examine the photographs and the film before I consider any payment.'

'Naturally.'

'As soon as possible.'

'Whenever you like. I can arrange . . .'

At this point several surprising things happened very quickly. A flash-bulb flared and, before Marc could find his wits let alone act, flared again. Duncliffe, camera at the ready, had obviously popped out from behind the carefully draped buttocks of one of Daumier's semi-classical ladies. More alarmingly, the gallery suddenly seemed to be full of policemen; in fact only five, but five gendarmes in an enclosed space can seem like an army. A Sergeant was saying, 'Monsieur Gérard, Mademoiselle Sorensen, I am arresting you on charges of extortion and blackmail. Anything you now say may be taken down and used in evidence against you.'

He nodded to his men. Joanna and Marc found themselves seized, and a second later both of them felt, for the first time in their young lives, the unpleasant sensation of cold steel being snapped into place around their wrists. And there was nothing remotely phoney about *this* manifestation of law and order.

Only then did Marc find words. He shouted, 'You have no proof. Only this man's word against ours.'

For answer, Duncliffe handed to the Sergeant his camera, a Polaroid, and Charles Foxley handed him the packet of cigarettes.

2

When they were led from the separate cells where they had been allowed a psychologically demoralizing half-hour of solitary reflection, these two objects were the first things they saw reposing on the desk of the Inspector of Police into whose office they were conducted.

The Inspector, a brisk, no-nonsense type of man, sat behind the desk examining them with interest. He pointed to two instant prints lying beside the Polaroid: the first of them showed Marc and Joanna talking earnestly to Charles Foxley, and the second, Marc and Joanna gaping at the camera in shock, which for obvious reasons Mr Foxley was not sharing. The Inspector opened the packet of cigarettes and extracted from it a small tape-recorder; he then pressed the Start button of a somewhat larger recorder which also sat on the desk. No further explanation was necessary.

Foxley's voice said, 'You want me to pay you for these photographs of my wife.'

Marc's voice said, 'Yes.'

'How much?'

'A million and a half dollars.'

It had not been a long conversation, and the policeman seemed to think they should be reminded of it all: right up to the sound of scuffling feet, gasps of astonishment, and 'Monieur Gérard, Mademoiselle Sorensen, I am arresting

you on charges of . . .' The Inspector switched off the
machine and spread his hands.

Joanna had lived for so long with the realization that
Marc's whole plan was insane and certain to lead to disaster,
and she had told him as much so frequently, that it came
as a surprise, when she glanced at him now, to see that the
same realization had only just hit him, leaving him defeated
and bereft. She couldn't have said with honesty that the
sight was purely displeasing because, however he might
have argued to the contrary, she still believed that blackmail
was a particularly unpleasant crime, and if he hadn't known
it before he certainly knew it at this moment.

As to his assertion that he only wanted the money to help
her make that first film she was always talking about . . .
Well, whether it was true or not, and she was inclined to
think it was, there was certainly no point in considering his
misplaced generosity now. At any rate, all the rage generated
by their battle of wills in Great-aunt Claudine's salon had
evaporated into thin air, and her heart went out to him in
his distress. She supposed, with the weary resignation which
so often visits women regarding their menfolk, that at least
she would be at his side to help and support him in whatever
lay ahead.

They had been taken; hoodwinked by a rich and powerful
man who had *become* rich and powerful because he was good
at hoodwinking people. Marc had known it, he had even
said it; the only thing he hadn't done was to take warning
from the knowledge. She sighed, thinking that if there was
any comfort to be found in the situation, it lay in the fact
that they had fallen into the hands of the police via a rich
Englishman rather than into the hands of Leo Nogaro and
his merry men.

The policeman now said, 'You realize the extreme serious-
ness of the charges which face you?'

Marc nodded mutinously. Joanna said, 'Yes, we do.'

'In due course you will be afforded access to legal advice.

Prior to that, I must ask you, Monsieur Gérard, to tell me where this evidence, the film, etcetera, is hidden.'

Marc remained silent, evidently clinging to some last waterlogged piece of wreckage. Impatiently, Joanna replied, 'In the baggage-check at the Gare St Charles.'

'We will go there at once and collect it.'

Sitting in the police car, Joanna realized, as she had been too alarmed to realize on their journey from the Palais de Longchamp to the Gendarmerie, that at last she felt physically safe: for the first time since Marc had read her that report on the deaths of Carlo César and his secretary. Admittedly they were up to their necks in every other kind of trouble, but in this one respect police custody had put an end to fear.

She stayed in the car with the driver and another gendarme, and wasn't even bothered by the curious faces which gazed in at her (something she'd better get used to anyway, there was going to be a lot of it) while Marc, escorted by the officer, went to collect the travel-bag. When she saw it in the policeman's hand she felt a touch of something like affection for it, remembering with what euphoric determination she had bought it at the airport gift-shop, stuffed it with newspaper, escaped by bus, feeling so pleased with herself. Pleased!

The police car shot away from the railway station, making clamorous use of its siren to slice a path through traffic which was beginning to build towards the rush-hour. Since she was sitting next to him, and it was no crime in any case, she put out a hand and laid it over Marc's fists which were tightly bunched together. He flashed her a look of almost desperate gratitude; the light brown eyes were still hard and fierce, but with the fierceness of a boy who has been whipped, knows he deserved it, but is still full of resentment.

He said, 'I'm sorry, Jeanne—and for those things I said. You were right all the time.'

Neither of them, encased in private mortification, realized

that they weren't returning to the Gendarmerie, but since the police adhered to their own mysterious routines, this could have meant anything; they were probably being taken to some other place of incarceration, pending interviews with the *juge d'instruction*, that all-seeing eye which is largely responsible for French law being fairer and more impartial than most others.

When the car suddenly swerved off the Boulevard Livon and into the forecourt of the Hôtel Pharo, both of them were surprised but not unduly so; it crossed Joanna's mind that perhaps Charles Foxley, chief witness for the prosecution as well as their victim, had the right to speak to them if he wished. The Inspector indicated that they should get out. He alone conducted them into the lobby. Duncliffe came forward to meet them.

He greeted his friendly contact-man and brother-under-the-skin, Inspector Brisson, with a smile. Joanna and Marc looked on in thunderstruck amazement while the Inspector handed this man the travel-bag, *their* travel-bag: while Duncliffe said, 'Thank you very much. I'm sure Mr Foxley will be most grateful.'

The Inspector seemed to know exactly what the remark meant. Even Marc and Joanna, coming out of shock, were beginning to have a pretty good idea of its meaning. Brisson nodded to Duncliffe and then, with unmistakable amusement in his eyes, to them. He turned back towards the police car.

Marc looked from the policeman's retreating back to the bag in Duncliffe's hand; he seemed to be having difficulty in speaking. 'What . . . ? That's . . Would you please . . .?'

Duncliffe said, 'Take it easy, Monsieur Gérard.'

'But . . .'

'All right, you've been had, double-crossed, call it what you like. This way.'

They followed him across the lobby to the elevators. In a quiet conversational tone, Duncliffe added, 'Take a tip from me—I discovered it years and years ago—never muck about with the rich, they win every time.'

Joanna grimaced, remembering Marc standing in his great-aunt's beautiful salon and crowing, 'Money, money, money—it's the miracle-worker. You're an American, you ought to know!' Well, the miracle had certainly been worked this time, and, like many another miracle before and since, it was a big fat con.

On the fourth floor Duncliffe knocked at a door: Suite D. It was well-known to Joanna since their female star had inhabited it all those æons ago when she had been a respectable Production Co-ordinator and not a common or garden crooked patsy. The door opened a few inches, and a hand, presumably Foxley's, took the travel-bag. Duncliffe escorted the pair onwards to his own room and let them into it. 'Here,' he said, 'is where we wait.'

During all this, Great-aunt Claudine returned from a shopping expedition which had followed the hairdresser's appointment. She found Henri, her more or less private chauffeur, waiting for her, his face as grave as Marguerite's habitually was. He told her how he had seen her great-nephew and his pretty girlfriend being led away from the Palais de Longchamp in handcuffs and bundled into a police car. He had made an heroic effort to follow and thereby learn their destination, but age, his own and that of the Peugeot, had defeated the intention.

Great-aunt Claudine was perfectly used to such drama in the type of newspaper she most preferred, but in one's own family . . .! She telephoned the police, and after barking up a number of wrong trees was finally connected to Inspector Brisson.

Yes, he informed her smoothly, it was perfectly true that Monsieur Gérard and Mademoiselle Sorensen had been requested to help the police with certain inquiries. Having done so, they had been released. No, he was sorry to say he had no idea where they now were.

They were still sitting in Duncliffe's bedroom at the Hôtel Pharo. Waiting. Nearly an hour had passed. There was little they could say to each other in front of a third person, particularly this one, and nothing they wanted to say to the large blond Englishman who was guarding them. When the telephone eventually buzzed and they were summoned into Charles Foxley's presence it was a relief: but a qualified one.

Duncliffe realized as soon as he saw his employer that during the hour, to be exact fifty-three minutes, a long time for looking at a single photograph, the alarming tension, so rigidly controlled, had passed the breaking-point. Whatever form the inevitable reaction had taken, Foxley was not betraying a trace of it, and only a man of Duncliffe's experience would even have suspected that an agonizing personal crisis had been confronted and conquered in this nondescript hotel suite.

The fact which Foxley turned to them as they entered was determinedly ordinary, determinedly blank, but . . . Yes, there was indeed a trace: a slight puffiness about the eyes which told Duncliffe that the man had wept, perhaps passionately and at length. Five minutes, then, for examining the woman in the photograph: twenty minutes of solitary grief: twenty-eight minutes for recovery, bathing the eyes in cold water, re-establishing the old composure. Duncliffe considered him an admirable person; it was a pleasure to have worked for him (most of his employers were very far from admirable) and he was sorry to have misjudged him, neither cold nor dull, sorry that the job was completed.

When Duncliffe had withdrawn, Charles Foxley examined the young man and the girl all over again, as if he had never seen them before. 'Sit down, I want to talk to you.'

They sat down. Both were struck by an odd kind of stillness in him: the stillness, Duncliffe could have told them, of complete exhaustion. The voice was very quiet, and there was not the faintest indication of any triumph: which in

some way made it easier for Marc to bear his next remark.
'You realize, of course, that I'm paying you nothing for your
evidence. A million and a half! When all that this charade
has cost me is a few thousand francs. You're lucky I'm not
prosecuting you—but remember, I have that tape-recording
and the pictures of you that go with it. If you don't behave
yourselves . . .' Obviously he didn't have to say any more;
that particular aspect was concluded.

'On the other hand I have to thank you for your intelligence, percipience. But for you I'd never have known . . .
what I now know. For this reason, and for others, I'm going
to tell you something—something I've never told anyone
else. It . . . It no longer matters to me, I am . . .' He glanced
away, and neither of them heard what word he used; it
could have been 'released'.

There was a long silence. The window was open; the
westering sun streamed in, filling the far end of the room
with golden light, but the three of them were not touched
by it, and Charles Foxley was merely a dark figure against
the glare, almost a silhouette.

'When that ransom demand was made—by telephone, a
man with a German accent, I . . . I naturally demanded to
speak to my wife, as proof that they were indeed holding
her. She spoke to me. She said she was being treated well,
but she sounded . . . terrified, and begged me to pay them
as soon as possible.' He shook his head over the memory.
'A year ago—it seems longer.

'I didn't go to Milan as the media believed. I spent a lot
of money to ensure they believed it. I went to Amsterdam
because that was what had been stipulated.

'In the meantime the money had been transferred to a
private bank, one I often used and could trust implicitly. A
million and a half dollars in cash, that was the agreement.
I was to put this money in a suitcase and place the suitcase
behind a telephone kiosk on the edge of a canal—I was to
make absolutely sure that the police were not present. That

wasn't difficult, I'd never told them who I was or why I was in their city.

'It wasn't a busy part of Amsterdam, and at the chosen time, eight o'clock on a Tuesday evening, there were few people about. I watched from the other side of the canal. I saw a man go to the place and take the suitcase. That night Melissa was returned to me. She was tired and under great strain. Understandably, as I thought then—even more understandably now I know the facts. I was delighted to see her, overjoyed.' He sat silent for a moment in his darkness, and then added, 'I loved her very much. She did not, at any time of our marriage, love me.'

There was something so intolerably bleak about this confession that Joanna had to look away from him. Marc's eyes, on the contrary, never left the older man's face, what could be seen of it. When Foxley renewed his narrative there was a change in him. He paused more often, searching for words; in view of what he had to tell, this struck neither of his listeners as surprising.

'You must understand, I was in Amsterdam alone. I trusted no one. *No one.* Her safe return was too important to me. That same night . . .' Obviously it cost him a great effort to complete this sentence. 'That same night, while I was asleep, she ran away, disappeared.'

Joanna let out a soft gasp. Marc ran a hand over his face and through his hair.

'If I spoke to you on the phone of . . . confidence-tricksters you will perhaps appreciate what I meant. I was the victim of . . . of a brutal confidence-trick. I had no proof of who had helped her perpetrate it, I still have no proof, but your photograph . . . confirms . . . seems to confirm what I always suspected—and in the past year I've spent a small fortune investigating the matter.'

He looked away from them towards the harbour and the sunlight. 'It's a strange thing—I often dream of that telephone-box by the canal. Yet it has no meaning.'

Again the controlled, finely-cut but unremarkable features reappeared in silhouette. 'I don't find pride an admirable quality, but . . . one is what one is—I confess to being a proud man. In Amsterdam, in those particular circumstances, I was the only person who knew what had happened—I discount . . . *them* for obvious reasons.

'Nothing, nothing on God's earth would have made me admit the truth. Not then. Not until now. I flew from the Netherlands to Milan. I appeared in public there—not much, just enough to attract the attention of the Italian Press. Then I flew back to London and told the story I'd prepared—that neither the kidnappers nor my wife had turned up at the appointed rendezvous. It was believed.'

There was another long silence; then he spread his hands as if that was the end of the story. Hesitantly Marc said, 'But you identified . . .'

'I identified the body of a woman who was not my wife. She was wearing one of my wife's dresses, her watch, some of her jewellery. The handbag contained my wife's credit-cards and passport, her car-keys . . .' He pressed both hands over his eyes as if expunging the sight. 'The hair,' he added, 'continues to grow after death. That woman's hair had been bleached blonde. Few people knew, as I did, that my wife was . . . is a natural blonde.'

Another silence; then, wearily, 'I don't expect you, anyone, to understand.'

They listened to the tinkling and rattling of yachts' rigging from the Old Port outside the window. Marc said, 'I certainly don't understand one thing—why have you told us all this?'

3

The woman who had been Melissa Foxley but now called herself Christina Neff was pacing around the pleasant living-room of the Villa Isabelle, furnished with antique

Provençal country pieces. The Nogaros, father and son, sat in two armchairs, looking not at her but across the terrace towards the Mediterranean and the crouched, sun-blasted, sea-blasted shapes of the offshore islands. She said, 'Well, for God's sake, how long are we going to sit here doing nothing?'

Benny Nogaro replied, 'We're not doing nothing. A lot of other people are looking for them now, and believe me, they'll be found.' It did not sound convincing even to himself, and it certainly didn't convince her.

'My trouble is, Benny, that I *don't* believe you.'

Silence. Both male faces averted.

'Jesus! Why can't you at least be honest? This isn't a big house, one can hear every damn word anyone says in it.'

'If one listens hard enough.'

'Certainly I've listened, it's the only way to find anything out, nobody ever tells you. Leo's screwed up your entire organization, it hardly exists any more. You're not going to grab those bloody kids because you *can't*.'

Leo's father gave her a malevolent glance. 'Picked the wrong man, didn't you?'

Without replying, she strode out of the shadowy room on to the terrace and was turned into a golden woman by the light of the setting sun. She was filled with a violent, almost physical desire to get away from these two men and this house: the desire for a new place and a new face seen across a room yet unknown: the first meeting of eyes which would lead to a logical conclusion in a new bed; the very idea made her heart beat faster. From behind her, as if he could read her thoughts, Benny said, 'You're free to go any time you like, Madame.'

She swung around on him furiously. 'I'm not leaving this villa until you've delivered your side of the bargain.'

'Then come in from that terrace, someone may be taking photographs.'

Leo sniggered, was still sniggering when she re-entered

the room. She leaned over and slapped his face as hard as she could. In a flash he was on his feet, hands about her beautiful throat; she staggered backwards, slipping and falling, the enraged man straddling her, but not in quite the manner which was her pleasure.

Benny Nogaro watched this act of mutual destruction with interest; he wondered how far Leo would go if he did not himself intervene. As things turned out, the telephone saved him the trouble.

'Nogaro.'

Marc knew at once that he was not talking to a young man; this was not the voice of Little Leo, and there was only one other Nogaro, the legendary one. He proceeded with caution: 'Monsieur Nogaro, my name's Gérard, Marc Gérard.'

Benny Nogaro's heart turned over. These days it required something quite exceptional to make it perform such tricks; but if he wasn't mistaken something exceptional had just occurred. 'Ah, I wondered when you'd ring.' His son and the woman were now very still, listening avidly.

The conversation which followed was more explicit than Marc's first conversation with Charles Foxley, but followed it so closely that a certain sense of unreality was generated.

'What exactly does this film show?'

'The film shows very little, but I've had the important frames enlarged—they show Mrs Charles Foxley on the roof-garden with your son.'

So they did know it all, names included. 'And you're proposing to sell them to me, correct?'

'Yes.'

'Very well, we must meet, I must take a look at your . . . merchandise. No doubt you have a place in mind.'

'On the Quai du Port there's a small bar, Le Bar des Moulins . . .'

'Which belongs to one of your relatives. A Madame Argenti if I'm not mistaken.'

'You're not mistaken.'

'At one time, when I was in that kind of business, Madame Argenti used to pay me a small sum weekly—in lieu of protection from undesirables, you understand.'

'Yes, she told me. The bar is closed tonight. We can meet there whenever you wish.'

Benny Nogaro glanced at the sea and the sky. In half an hour it would be dark, and darkness would be necessary. 'In one hour.'

'Okay, one hour. And Monsieur Nogaro? Please bring Mrs Foxley with you—her interest in this is as strong as yours, maybe stronger. If you don't want to pay she might encourage you.'

Benny Nogaro laughed; he felt for the first time in a painful twenty-four hours that he cold afford to do so. Luck was undoubtedly on his side again. It was a pity the young man had to be killed; he had a brain and guts, more of both than Leo, however much one loved him; a boy like that could prove useful in the new empire which must be built on the ruins of the old one. Impossible, alas.

'Very well, Monsieur Gérard, you're calling the hand. Bar des Moulins, eight o'clock.'

He replaced the receiver and looked at the woman who was massaging her neck; there would be unpleasant bruises. She gave him a curt nod of satisfaction and turned out of the room without even glancing at Leo. Benny Nogaro, however, directed at his son an omniscient look and saw that he was actually preening himself on having assessed the situation correctly; he even said, 'I knew they'd come to us.'

Oh God, what a fool the boy was! Could he ever be taught? 'Leo?'

'Yes, Father.'

'You still have that motor-yacht?'

'Yes, Father.'

'Can you trust the crew?'

'Of course.' Affronted. Meaning: What kind of an idiot do you think I am?

'Absolutely?'

Before the searching scrutiny of those black eyes which knew him so well, the young man's certainty faltered. 'Two of them anyway.'

'I want her standing by with those two men, only those two, at the south end of the Quai du Port. I want the bodies dropped fifty-five kilometres due south of Toulon, beyond the six-thousand-metre deep. Do you understand that?'

'Yes, Father.'

'Repeat it.'

Leo did so, incorrectly. Benny sighed. '*Fifty*-five kilometres south of Toulon. Any nearer and it's too shallow. Make the necessary arrangements. Nylon sailcloth, nylon cord, metal weighting—not concrete, Leo, metal.'

'Yes, Father.'

4

When Joanna and Marc arrived at the Bar des Moulins they found Madame Argenti on the telephone. She was wearing a purple and lime-green flowered dress with merely a touch of red to pick up the colour of her hair. She said, 'Wait—they've just walked in.' And to Marc, 'It's your Great-aunt Claudine.'

He grimaced at Joanna as he took the receiver.

'What in heaven's name are you doing, child? Am I to understand you were actually arrested?'

'Yes. But everything's all right now.'

'I'm not too sure about that! A *very* peculiar individual came here, saying he was a friend of yours and asking if I knew where you were. I gather Madame Argenti received a caller too.'

'Who was he?'

'Not the type who gives his name. Considering that photo-

graph of yours, I suspect he had something to do with
Monsieur Nogaro.'

'You didn't tell him anything?'

'Dear boy, my experience of such things may be at
second-hand, unlike yours, but I'm remarkably bright for
my age. I told him you were in England visiting Henriette
and your Uncle James.'

'Thank you, Great-aunt.'

'You may thank me by coming here and telling me the
whole story as soon as you can.'

'We will.'

'My regards to charming Jeanne, and please take care of
yourselves.'

He replaced the receiver to find yet another female relative
eyeing him with concern. 'I hope,' said Madame Argenti,
'that you know what you're doing.'

'I hope so too.'

The bar seemed ominously quiet without the usual bois-
terous conversation and laughter of its clientele, without the
fidget and flicker of the pin-ball machines, the cries of rage
or triumph from the miniature football-field. Madame had
been willing enough to pin to her door the notice, 'Apologies
—Closed Tonight, Friday 20th', particularly as she had
been promised payment to match her usual Friday take; she
would now change into something comfortable, and settle
down to watch an old Alain Delon film on television: or
rather, that was what she intended to do if she could stop
worrying about these two children.

There had been no point in concealing from her the fact
that they were meeting the Nogaros, father and son, in her
establishment; she would find out anyway via the grapevine;
already she knew that Benny Nogaro was back in town, as
did the greater part of Marseille.

'Well . . .' She looked around the old place, hoping that
no Nogaro enemy would try tossing a bomb into it. This
had happened before, in a bar near the market; but Benny

had got wind of the plot and had arranged to hold his meeting elsewhere: which hadn't prevented the bar from being wrecked. Of course she was insured against such acts of men, though not those of God, but her 'cousin' and his pretty girl could take out no such insurance on themselves; moreover, they wouldn't listen to her advice if she gave it to them, and she supposed that this was just as well: if young people always took the advice of old people the world would come to a standstill. She shrugged and left them to their own crazy schemes, whatever they might be. The time was now seven-forty.

When she had gone, Marc and Joanna looked at each other. She said, 'No, I don't like it. But I've never liked any part of it from the word Go.'

He said, 'Cognac, that's what we need.'

He had barely poured out the two glasses before the telephone rang, making them both jump. It was Madame Argenti. She told Marc that the bar was already being cased; on her way out she'd seen two of Leo Nogaro's men whom she knew well by sight; they'd been inspecting the back entrance. The time was seven fifty-two.

It was a little uncanny, sitting there together under the ugly strip-lighting, holding hands and drinking Courvoisier, while the rats skittered around them in the drains and under the floorboards, making sure the place was safe for King Rat and the Crown Prince. On the strength of it they drank a little more brandy. While they were doing so, one of Madame's more elderly customers, who had clearly visited other bars, looked in at them and withdrew at Marc's request.

Eight o'clock came and went. At five minutes past, they heard cars stopping outside; car doors slammed. Then Zizi came into the bar with two of his men; he gave them an unfriendly glance. There were few places to search beyond the single *toilette*, a cupboard known as 'the store', and the refrigerator, but these were duly searched.

Only then did Zizi open the door to admit, first Melissa Foxley, looking cool and beautiful and soignée, with a scarf hiding the bruises on her neck. Next came the perpetrator of the bruises, arrogant and excessively good-looking in white, but unable to meet anyone's eye directly. Benny entered last, wearing his most Imperial air, not as Roman in the Bar of the Windmills as it was in Tunis where the djelabah so greatly enhanced it.

As far as Joanna was concerned an old and well-known sense of unreality came into the bar with them. She recalled the first time she had met big movie-stars off the set: could these little, fractious humans really be the sacred monsters who had lorded it over her youth, over her whole life? Here and now, could these three people be the monsters who had been haunting her and hunting her for the past three days? It wasn't possible that this charming woman in the immaculate suit had actually committed such a repulsive crime, tortured her husband so callously; nor that this beautiful young man had aimed a gun at fat and jolly Carlo and blown his head off; nor that the benign elderly man in the crumpled suit was responsible for the agony of uncountable heroin addicts all over the world, and paid his bills out of the earnings of a thousand whores.

Why did none of it show in their faces? Things like that *had* to show on people's faces. Joanna Sorensen was growing up fast; had been doing so by leaps and bounds during the past seventy-two hours.

The woman sat down at a small table where, pointedly, there was no room for the two men, thus distancing herself not only from them but from the entire proceeding. Benny Nogaro nodded to Marc and Joanna, noting their apprehension, noting how very young they both were: much too young to be dying within the next fifteen to thirty minutes, but that was their business. He sat behind a larger table, his son next to him.

Marc gestured towards the well-stocked bar. 'May I offer you something?'

'No,' said Benny. 'Get on with the business.'

'Yes, please,' said Mrs Foxley in her coolest voice. 'I'd adore a Perrier.'

Joanna recognized the gambit and even admired it; at the same time she wondered what it could conceivably be like to be Melissa Foxley. They both belonged to the female sex of the genus *Homo sapiens*, and as it happened they were both beautiful, but beyond that lay a yawning chasm of disparity and incomprehension.

When Marc had dispensed the Perrier, Benny Nogaro said, 'All right. You have pictures of my son and this lady on the roof-garden of 10 Rue du Palais.'

'Yes.'

'And you propose to sell them to me.'

'Yes.'

'How much?'

'For the enlargements, for the only print of the film, and for the negative, one and a half million dollars.'

Mrs Foxley sipped her Perrier. Only an hour ago it had looked as if this whole deal had capsized on top of her. Now, once again, it had regained its former balance and was entirely to her advantage. One and a half million dollars, the same old sum! It was amusing really. She smiled.

Benny said, 'You think they're worth that much?'

'I know they are as well as you do.'

'Very well, we won't argue about it. Show me the enlargements.'

Marc glanced at the clock. Seventeen minutes past eight. 'You must think I'm a fool, Monsieur Nogaro. If I hand them to you now, in this bar, your son puts a bullet through my head. Both our heads.'

Benny leaned forward. 'You mean to say you've got me all the way down here, *me*, to tell me you don't have the proof?'

'It can be here within ten minutes.'

'Then get it. God, how I hate amateurs!'

The time was now eight-twenty. Marc went to the telephone, but as he lifted the receiver, before he could even
begin to dial, there was the sound of voices from the street.
He paused, glancing over his shoulder.

The door opened and Zizi came in, all apologies. He had
obviously been told to keep well away, out of earshot, and
on no account to interrupt.

Leo said, 'Zizi, get out!'

'But there's this man . . .'

Benny groaned. 'I thought I gave orders . . .'

'He says you'll want to see him once I tell you his name.
Monsieur Foxley—Monsieur Charles Foxley.'

The silence was extraordinary. Thick and heavy, it spread
over the room like newly-mixed cement. Then there was the
grating of a chair on the tiled floor. Melissa Foxley was
standing up unsteadily, supporting herself on the wall. On
entering the bar she had looked perhaps twenty-seven, ten
years less than her actual age; suddenly she looked a good
ten years older than that age. Little Leo also stood up. Both
of them were staring at Nogaro Senior whose expression
had barely changed in spite of the fact that he now realized
he had walked into a trap. And he had called the boy an
amateur! 'Is Mr Foxley alone?'

'No, there's a big Englishman with him.'

'Bring him in. His friend can . . .'

Melissa Foxley cried out, 'No! Benny, no!'

He gave her a black, brooding look, an Arab look. She
caught her breath, because she had not realized until this
moment, had never truly realized, how much he hated and
despised her. 'You think we're in a position to keep him
hanging around out there?'

She shook her head and glanced away from the hatred;
the floor seemed to be tilting and lurching under her feet.
Benny turned from her and said to Zizi, 'His friend can stay
outside.'

'He wants that anyway, Mr Nogaro. I mean, he wants to come in alone.'

Joanna had moved closer to Marc. His fingers found hers; she clutched them.

Zizi was holding the door open so that for a moment the sound of the yachts in the port, rattle of halliards and slap of water on hull, was loud, even deafening. Then Charles Foxley came forward out of darkness and stepped into the bar. He was pale and almost violently calm. Zizi closed the door. Foxley paused just inside it and stared at his wife; he simply went on looking at her for what could have been a full minute, two minutes; no doubt for her it seemed like all eternity. Then he wrenched his eyes away from her and moved forward, nodding to Joanna and Marc. He said, 'How about a large Scotch? Equal water, no ice.'

Joanna, pouring it, relieved to be doing something familiar and practical, found that her hands were shaking uncontrollably. While she was thus engaged, Charles Foxley sat on one of the bar-stools and looked at the three people confronting him. He said, 'I find this . . . distasteful beyond words. But it has to be done, and I don't propose to waste any time.' He spoke only to Benny Nogaro. 'You've obviously guessed by now that I hold all the evidence.'

The other man was looking at Marc and Joanna. Foxley understood his meaning. 'I told them everything—I had to, since I wanted them to help me.'

Benny nodded. 'How do I know this so-called evidence even exists?'

'You know, Monsieur Nogaro. It's not a matter worth discussing—you know it exists.'

Benny sighed and shrugged. Foxley thanked Joanna for the Scotch and downed half of it in a couple of gulps. Then: 'I must tell you that I didn't pay one and a half million for it—and as one businessman to another I see no reason why you should pay either.'

Benny Nogaro's regard became more concentrated. He

sensed fair play, even charity, and they above all were the two things he most distrusted in another businessman.

'I'm informed,' said Foxley, 'that your son's motor-yacht is berthed just along the quay. It's my opinion that if these two young people had been in a position to hand you that film their bodies would already be on it, heading out to sea.'

'That's neither here nor there.' He didn't add 'now' but it was implicit.

'I don't agree. The fact that you were prepared to kill them—please correct me if I'm wrong—even though you would by then have been in possession of their evidence, proves that you were frightened of *them*. Of what they know. That hasn't changed, so I take it you're still frightened.'

Benny said nothing: which amounted to agreement.

'You needn't be. They won't talk for the same reason that none of you will talk—I'm in the happy position of being able to blackmail the lot of you. And, Monsieur Nogaro, I wouldn't hesitate to release my information if any harm comes to either of them. You understand me.'

Silence. Foxley allowed himself the ghost of a smile. 'In fact, I think we can say that I hold all the cards in this particular hand.'

'Forget the youngsters—let's talk business.'

'No, I can't forget them. They've performed a great service for me. Their actions have, yes, set my mind at rest. It's not I think beyond *your* comprehension—' meaning that he considered it entirely beyond the comprehension of his wife and Leo—'that for a whole year I have . . . suffered a very great deal.'

Benny nodded. Why pretend to himself that he had ever condoned anything which his son and the woman had done? In his own way he too had suffered because of them. He found that he could respect Charles Foxley.

'In my opinion,' Foxley continued, 'this boy and girl deserve payment. They deserve to be paid by the person who has most to lose were I to hand those photographs to the public prosecutor.' The glacial green eyes moved to his wife's face.

She tried a laugh, but failed; said, 'You're being absurd. I don't have that kind of money and you know it.'

'I know that only a year ago you robbed me of one and a half million dollars. If you've spent it all so quickly, you're even more extravagant than you used to be. In any case, I'm sure your handsome young friend will help you—or did he play his part entirely for . . . love?' Not even glancing at Leo, he turned again to his father.

'Monsieur Nogaro, I don't have to spell this out to a man of your experience. Publication of that evidence will merely make *me* look a fool—my only apparent crime is an incorrect identification, and they'd have a hard time proving it wasn't an honest mistake. On the other hand your son's crimes include extortion and faked kidnapping, not to mention two recent murders in this city and a third in Germany. What other charges might be brought against him you know better than I. In any case I doubt if you'd ever see him again, except behind bars, and I'm told you're fond of him.'

Benny Nogaro remained silent. Everything the Englishman had said was, alas, perfectly true; in this particular hand he did indeed hold all the cards. A great deal of bitter experience had taught him how to lose, if not gracefully then with minimum stress to his own system. Philosophically speaking, he would have agreed wholeheartedly with Joanna's father; 'Accept what you must' was a maxim which could be shared by the Connecticut academic and the Provençal gangster. He said, 'Very well, Monsieur Foxley, I agree to your terms.'

'Good. And since your son's life depends on it, I'm sure I can leave it to you to see that the necessary sum, one and a half million dollars, is transferred from my wife's account, wherever she now holds it, into one of my accounts of which these are the details.' He handed Benny Nogaro a typewritten slip. 'We all know that the transaction can be completed tomorrow. If it isn't, I shall consider giving the police that photograph of her and your son.'

He looked for the last time at the woman he had once loved so much. 'Don't waste time arguing, just do it—or spend the rest of your life in prison, whichever you prefer.' He nodded to himself. 'I think that discharges the only debts I owe.'

He then finished his Scotch, placed the glass neatly in Madame Argenti's sink, and turned towards Joanna and Marc. 'I can give you a lift, there's a car outside.'

When they had gone, after the sound of their departure had dwindled to silence, the ordinary noises of the city crept back into the shabby bar: traffic, yachts in the harbour, a police car driving up the Canebière, siren yowling.

Benny Nogaro sat lumped in the chair from which he had never moved, dark eyes withdrawn, deep in thought. Charles Foxley was that interesting phenomenon, rare in his own milieu but none the less instantly recognizable, a man of his word. He would only use the evidence if his terms were disregarded, and there was no reason why this should happen. Therefore Leo, for what he was worth, was safe: safer than he deserved to be.

Obviously he must himself resume direction of Marseille. This meant that Louis Armand could remain in Nice and that Leo could be sent there for corrective training; if he was lucky, that's to say a little more intelligent than he appeared to be, he could perhaps take over . . . well, Cannes. Not much of a place, but exactly the kind of thing he'd fancy. What else was there? Oh yes, the money.

He glanced up at Melissa Foxley, who was no longer looking fiftyish but had not by any means regained her former gloss; he didn't doubt, however, that she would presently do so, women were extraordinary in so many ways.

He said, 'I know you bank in Switzerland, I've forgotten where.'

'Benny, please listen to me—I can't possibly . . .' It was his eyes which stopped her; she had always known that he didn't care for her very much, but she was completely taken aback by the blank, Arab emptiness of this stare which nullified her outright; to him she wasn't even a person, let alone a beautiful woman: merely a counter on a gaming table, like Leo.

To hell with him anyway, to hell with both of them! Of course the present situation would necessitate a slight change of plan. Not that she would be by any means penniless; however carelessly she had behaved during her years as Mrs Charles Foxley, however drunk or stoned she might occasionally have been, she had never omitted to subtract a little something from her husband's wealth, weekly, sometimes daily. She would still go to the Americas, but no longer, alas, as a lady of independent means; another marriage might be called for; law-courts in the United States were notoriously generous when it came to alimony, and next time she'd make damn sure that *she* was the one who had grounds for divorce—there were obviously ways of arranging such things . . .

'I asked you a question, Madame, please answer it. Where is your Swiss Bank?'

She shrugged, accepting defeat. Temporary defeat. 'Zürich.'

'There's a plane around eight o'clock tomorrow morning —we'll be on it.'

5

It had been Joanna's wish to travel from Marseille to Paris on the TGV. After all, any old person anywhere in the world could go by jet, but a train that went 170 m.p.h., that was something else! In fact, the ride proved to be so smooth and noiseless that the speed was barely noticeable.

Marc waited until they had eaten their picnic lunch and had finished their picnic wine, and were reclining side by side in somnolent First Class comfort, waited indeed until the train was at maximum speed between Lyon and Paris, before handing her the little slip of paper: 'The following sum has been paid into the account of Joanna Elizabeth Sorensen at the Bank of . . . $1,500,000.'

She knew she was gaping at it, lost for words, and this was ridiculous because they had discussed the money, in the abstract, more than once since that weird neon-lit exorcism in the Bar des Moulins; they had even managed to avoid, but only just, yet another ideological battle concerning the rights and wrongs of accepting it.

Marc laughed at her expression. She was perfectly aware of the fact that it must indeed be comical. She managed to say, 'You never told me it had come.'

'I hoped I'd surprise you. Seems I have.'

'I didn't . . . think it'd be this quick.'

'When a man like Foxley wants a thing done quickly, he gets it.'

Try as she might, it seemed that she couldn't leave well enough (if that's what it was) alone; might never in all her life be able to do so: '*Why* did he do it, Marc?'

'He was grateful to us.'

'*This* grateful?'

'Apparently. He loved her—can't you imagine what he went through during that year? The relief of knowing the truth, however awful it was?'

She nodded, not entirely sure that she comprehended this male reasoning.

'He said that if we need more, when it comes to making your film, we must go to him, not mess around with Studios and Networks.'

'He said that?'

'Yes.' He wondered why a slow colour had crept over her

face; he had never seen her blush before. It was because she
could hear her own voice shouting, 'You're a dumb, greedy,
stupid peasant who can't see further than the end of his
nose.' She held out the piece of paper and said, 'It's yours
really, Marc. I mean, you're the one who . . . who . . .'

'Who was the crook.'

'I didn't mean that.'

'Didn't you?' He kissed her cheek gently and laughed
again. 'No. I always wanted it for you.' And, misreading
her hesitation: 'Of course it will have to be a very low
budget, good actors, no stars, but everybody has to start in
a small way.'

The reality of what she was holding in her hand suddenly
arose like the big wave which takes you by surprise and
sweeps over you, leaving you breathless. She too began to
laugh. 'I can't, it's ridiculous, I don't even have a story.'

'Oh yes you do.'

LAP DISSOLVE TO:

1. EXT. STREET IN LOS ANGELES. DAY.   1.

Across the busy thoroughfare is seen a movie-theatre:
not by any means one of the city's biggest, but an
important one.

WORKMEN are changing the title of what's showing, re-
arranging large metal letters above the marquee:

        A O N S   R P   O D
              A SS O

2. REVERSE ANGLE—JOANNA AND MARC   2.

They are standing on the other side of the street, staring.

CAMERA moves in, among traffic, to TWO-SHOT, revealing that she looks apprehensive, he buoyant.

> JOANNA
> I keep remembering Monsieur
> Laurent, those awful lawyers.

> MARC
> Jeanne! It all happens in
> Naples, doesn't it? Nothing
> to do with Marseille.

Joanna nods, but uncertainly.

> MARC (continuing)
> Nobody can do a thing with-
> out incriminating themselves.
> Specially Benny Nogaro.

> JOANNA
> I guess you're right.

> MARC
> And Foxley okayed the script.

Joanna glances back at the theatre, and what she sees banishes her uncertainty, replacing it with a smile of pure delight.

> JOANNA
> Oh Marc, look!

3. RESUME SHOT TO THEATRE   3.

The men have sorted out the letters over the marquee. The title now reads:

A JOANNA SORENSEN PRODUCTION

'L A S T   S H O T'

FADE OUT. THE END.